VOYAGE
TO
VENNING ROAD

A tale of enduring love, a guilty secret, and ultimate tragedy,
set in Colonial Malaya and post-Edwardian England,
and based on a true-life story.

MARGARET S GOLDTHORP

ISBN: 978-1-326-66337-7

PublishNation
www.publishnation.co.uk

CONTENTS

Part I

Chapter 1

On Tuesday 11th October 1910, Joss boarded the Great Northern Railway train to Bradford and Leeds at Kings Cross station and settled himself into an empty compartment. His ship had docked earlier that morning at Tilbury and, after saying farewell to his companions on the long voyage and seeing to the despatch up to Yorkshire of his trunk, he had boarded the express train to London. Now he was on the last leg of his long journey, with a whole year ahead of him in England before returning to the Federated Malay States.

He had bought a newspaper at the station and started to read it, but found his thoughts wandering. He was returning home, but not to the home he had left seven years earlier. He had spent most of his childhood in the Almondbury area of Huddersfield, with his widowed mother and older brother, William. Now, his mother was dead, that house had been vacated, and he would be staying with his brother and sister-in-law and their three young children in Heckmondwike. He had known Theresa when she was William's fiancee, so she was not a stranger, but he had yet to meet the three children. Joss Donald (named after him but always called Donald) was now five years old, Mabel, three and the baby, Leslie, just over a year.

One of the first things he would do, once he had settled in, was to visit his mother's grave. She had died when he had been in Malaya only a month or so and it had been impossible to return home in time for the funeral. William had sent him a detailed account of the service and he could still vividly remember reading it in the privacy of his room in the cadets' bungalow in Seremban, his grief at her sudden death still very raw. His new friends and colleagues, aware of his loss, had been kind and sympathetic, but it had still been a very bad time.

He had also missed Will's marriage to Theresa, which had taken place later that year, but another long letter, with accompanying photographs, had described this happy event in detail. As the children arrived in speedy succession, further photos followed, showing them in various stages of development. He had brought the latest pictures with him and had shown them to some of his fellow passengers on the ship. One or two had commented that, if he were lucky enough to find a wife on this period of long leave, he would before long have children of his own.

It was customary for men working in the Malayan Civil Service to use their first long leave back in England, after the initial tour of duty which lasted six or seven years, to find a lady they wished to marry, and either have the wedding in England before they returned or arrange for their intended bride to follow later, to get married in Malaya. Beach weddings were quite popular amongst the Europeans. However, it was easier for a lot of the men to do this than it would be for him. They would return to upper or upper-middle class families and would socialise with the unmarried daughters of their parents' friends. In those circles, it was not unheard of for a girl to marry someone working in the Colonies and go to live out East. His background was much more humble and provincial, and even if Theresa had some unmarried girlfriends she could introduce him to, their families would probably view with horror the idea of their daughters going to live in the tropics.

Despite the fact that he was now thirty years old, his experience of women was fairly limited. He had won a scholarship to a select all boys grammar school, and from there a scholarship to Oxford. At Oxford, the men greatly outnumbered the women, who were in any case sequestered in women-only colleges. He had spent a year in London after graduating, attending language, law and other courses at the School of Oriental Studies in Finsbury Circus and taking his initial exams for the Malayan Civil Service. Some of his fellow students had introduced him to girls they knew, but at that stage there was no point in contemplating marriage, even if he had fallen in love, as the MCS only employed single men for the initial tour of duty. Once that had been completed, cadets had earned the right to have married quarters allocated and their wife's passage to Penang paid for.

During his spells of working in Kuala Lumpur and other large towns, he had enjoyed a busy social life, which included women, but the young single ones were in short supply and there was considerable competition for their company. Whilst in the capital, in common with other European bachelors, he had periodically availed himself of the services provided by the girls in the Japanese brothels in Petaling Street, but he regarded this as a poor substitute for a loving relationship. When posted out to the more remote districts, female company was a rarity. Some men took Malayan mistresses, but this was frowned upon by the service.

His reverie was interrupted by the train grinding to a halt, followed by the clanking of engines. They had arrived in Grantham, where they would be delayed for several minutes, whilst the engines were changed. He unpacked his lunch and started to eat. As he did so, the compartment door opened and a middle-aged woman entered, stowed her case overhead, settled herself into her seat and smiled at the pleasant looking, fair haired young man opposite.

"How far are you going?" she asked.

"Dewsbury."

"I'm going on to Bradford. Are we in the right part of the train? I believe it divides at Wakefield."

"Yes, I think we're alright here," Joss told her.

"Are you from Dewsbury?" she asked.

"Huddersfield, originally."

"Where do you live now, then?"

"Malaya."

Her eyes widened at this. "So, are you home for a holiday?"

"Yes, I've got extended leave."

"How long since you were last home?"

"Seven years."

"Your family must have missed you - your mother will be so happy to have you home!"

"My mother's dead, and I never knew my father, but I have a brother and he now has a family. I have two nephews and a niece whom I have not yet met."

"Oh, it will be nice for you to get to know them!" she said, beaming.

After a short period of silence, during which Joss finished his sandwich, she asked.

"What's it like out in Malaya, then? It must be hot!"

"Yes, and humid. But you get used to the climate after a while."

In response to her further questions, he found himself telling her about life in Malaya, both in Kuala Lumpur and other places where he had been posted. He described the houses they lived in, usually built on stilts, and the varied nature of the work, particularly out in the districts, where a District Officer performed a wide range of functions, including presiding in court as a magistrate. He spoke about the social life in Kuala Lumpur, mentioning the well-appointed Selangor club where all the Europeans congregated, and being invited to curry *tiffin* (lunch) on Sundays at the homes of friends. He told her about playing cricket, tennis and football in the humid heat, and emphasised the camaraderie which existed amongst the Europeans. He made her laugh with his description of the bathing and sanitary arrangements - which a lot of his gentler bred colleagues had found very primitive at first, but to which he had fairly quickly adapted after a childhood in a house with an outside

4

lavatory and a tin bath in the scullery. She shuddered with horror as he told her the measures they had to take in order to prevent ants getting into their food stores, and he described the luxury of having servants; a married couple would often have half a dozen staff, indoor and outdoor, and even bachelors like himself shared three or four servants, including a cook and a houseboy, with their housemates.

"So, you're not married then?" she asked.

"No."

"Are there English women out there?"

"Some, but most of them are married. There are not enough young single ones to go round! A lot of the chaps get married whilst home on leave."

"So, do you have a sweetheart waiting here for you?"

"Afraid not."

They relapsed into silence. After a little while, he asked her politely if she lived in Bradford. She said that she did and proffered details of her own family, which consisted of her husband and four grown children.

"My Betty would maybe be the right age for you, but she's already courting - and anyway, I wouldn't want her to go off to live in Malaya!"

"No, I expect a lot of parents would take that view, especially in Yorkshire. In the Home Counties, where a lot of my colleagues come from, it's less unusual."

"So, you'll have your work cut out then, if you want to find a wife," she grinned, and he smiled ruefully back.

Eventually, the train pulled into Dewsbury station and Joss stood, pulled his case down from the rack, and said good bye to his fellow passenger. He made his way to the tram stop, where he did not have too long to wait for a tram destined for Heckmondwike. Once there, he had to ask directions to Cambridge Street, where William now lived, following his promotion to manager of the music shop where

5

he worked. In the miniscule front garden of the square, stone, semi-detached house, a small boy and even smaller girl were playing. They looked up as he pushed open the gate.

"Are you our Uncle Joss?" the boy asked. He looked a little like William as a boy, Joss thought.

"I am. You must be Donald. And you're Mabel," he added, turning to the pretty little girl who was looking up at him shyly.

Donald ran inside the house, calling out to his mother that Uncle Joss had arrived. An attractive brown-haired young woman appeared in the doorway, with a smile of welcome. Joss greeted her with a hesitant peck on the cheek.

"Come in, get yourself settled," she said. "You must be ready for a cup of tea. I'll put the kettle on."

"Will not home yet?"

" No, not for another couple of hours. Donald has only just got home from school. Sit yourself down. Do you want something to eat or did you eat on the train. How was your journey?"

He replied to her questions and sank into a chair in the cosy, homely back room, which doubled as living room and kitchen and had a large cooking range. Donald and Mabel positioned themselves on either side of him.

"Will you tell me all about Malaya?" Donald asked.

"Yes, of course - anything you want to know. And how are you liking school; you've only just started, haven't you?"

"It's alright, I suppose."

"We've put you in the front room," Theresa said. "There's a settee in there which opens out into a bed. When Will gets home, you and he can put it up together - it's a bit awkward. Is that all your luggage?"

He explained that his trunk was on its way.

"Oh, well, there'll be room for that at the foot of the bed and you can put things on it."

"I hope I'm not putting you out too much. I'll be paying my way and I won't be here absolutely the whole time; I have to be in London during April to do some exams."

"Of course you are not putting us out! You are Will's only brother and I know he has missed you. He's been so looking forward to your visit - and so have I - and the children have been really excited! Oh, you haven't met Leslie yet! He's been having his afternoon nap, but I'll fetch him down."

She returned with the baby and deposited him on Joss' lap.

"This is our Uncle Joss, Leslie," Donald told him. "He lives in another country."

The baby appeared unimpressed and squirmed to get down. Theresa put him in his playpen in the corner of the room, whereupon he started to cry.

"He's always crying!" Donald said scornfully.

After he had drunk his tea, Theresa showed Joss the bureau drawers she had cleared for him in the front room, and he unpacked his case. Despite the warm welcome he had received, he suddenly felt rather disoriented. This was so different from coming home to his mother's house from Oxford for the holidays. He had belonged there. Now, he felt there was no one place he could really call home, either in England or Malaya, where cadets were moved regularly from one area to another.

He shook off his uncharacteristic bout of melancholy and returned to the other room. He showed Donald and Mabel some photographs of Malaya, including one of people riding elephants across a river, which they found very funny. He told them he had brought presents for them all, but that they were packed in his trunk, which would arrive in a day or two.

After a while, they heard the outer door open.

"That'll be Daddy," Donald said, and ran out into the hall, closely followed by Mabel. "Daddy, Uncle Joss is here!"

William came into the room and Joss rose from his chair, and moved towards him. The brothers looked quite alike, although William had a more serious demeanour. They started to shake hands, as was customary, then thought better of it and embraced each other.

"It's so good to see you!" they both said, more or less in unison, and then laughed.

Over tea - a Yorkshire high tea, which Joss realised how much he had missed - the ice was thoroughly broken as the brothers caught up with each other's news since their last exchange of letters. Donald and Mabel could scarcely get a word in, despite their best endeavours. After the meal had been cleared away, and Joss had dried the dishes for Theresa, she went upstairs with the children, to get them washed and ready for bed, Joss having promised to read them their bedtime story. The house had the luxury of an indoor bathroom.

"What are your plans for the next few days? " William asked. "I will be free from dinnertime Saturday and all day Sunday, except for church, so we can spend some time together then."

"That'll be good. Tomorrow, I'm going to Mum's grave."

"Yes, of course. You could take some fresh flowers from the garden. Theresa will cut some for you."

The next morning, Joss took the train from the nearby station into Huddersfield and then a tram to the cemetery. He knew where his mother's grave was, as she had been buried with his father and he and Will had often accompanied her there when they were children. His father had died when he was just two years old and Will not yet four and Joss had no memory of him. He arranged the flowers carefully in the stone jar, taking out the existing dying ones, and read the simple inscriptions: 'William Goldthorp 1844 to 1882' and 'Martha Goldthorp 1844 to 1904'. There was no-one else in that part of the cemetery, so he allowed himself to talk aloud to his mother, telling her how very sorry he was not to have been able to say goodbye and see her laid to rest. When he finally left the graveside, he felt as though a burden had been lifted from him.

The next few months passed very pleasantly. He looked up old school friends - mostly married with several children - reacquainted himself with his old haunts, got to know Donald and Mabel and took them out to the park and other places, and spent many convivial hours with his brother. He also made himself useful by doing some work in their back garden and some minor handyman jobs around the house.

They spent Christmas with Theresa's family, the Mallinsons, in Lockwood, Hudddersfield. She was one of seven surviving siblings. Her two younger brothers, Crossland and Ewart, were not married and Joss enjoyed some jolly evenings out with them in local hostelries, including on New Year's Eve. They lived with their widowed mother and two of their older sisters, Sarah and Edith, who were also still single, but, although they were only a few years older than he was, Joss could not see either of them as sweetheart material. The other sister, Mary, and brother, George, were both married with children.

Joss made arrangements for his stay in London in April, booking lodgings and contacting some old friends from university and a couple of colleagues from Malaya who were also on leave, with a view to meeting them while he was there. He was due to take his next set of Federated Malay States Civil Service exams, which, if passed, would pave the way for being moved up a grade, with an increase in salary and privileges.

Shortly before he was due to leave, William suggested that they book a short cruise around the Scottish Western isles for late May or June; just for the two of them.

"We thought of doing that once before, remember?" he said, "but it never materialised."

"Will Theresa not mind, leaving her alone with the children?"

"No, I think she'll be alright about it. It will only be for a week or ten days and it's only for this year; it's not something I'll be making a habit of!"

So the holiday was decided upon and booked, before Joss departed for London. He enjoyed his few weeks there and thought he had probably passed the exams, which he had found quite easy.

~ * ~

They left for Scotland at the beginning of June, travelling by train up to Oban the day before the cruise sailed. Donald & Mabel had been disappointed that they could not come with them; Donald's school term was still in progress, but he did not regard that as a good reason.

On the boat, the first evening, they found themselves sharing a table with a mother and daughter, also from Yorkshire. The older lady's name was Eliza Healey and her daughter - who was of an age with Joss and William - was called Gladys. Gladys was very attractive: slender but shapely, with brown eyes and abundant dark hair. They lived in Brighouse and Eliza's husband owned a factory there. After the initial introductions, Eliza and William fell into conversation together, while Joss talked to Gladys. Having told her he was on leave from Malaya, he then responded to her questions about life there and she was fascinated by the picture he portrayed.

Gladys lived at home with her parents, brother and cousin. The three men all worked in her father's factory but she did not have a job outside the home and often felt that life was passing her by. She had been courting once for a couple of years and had thought they might marry, but he had eventually married someone else. She was not particularly heartbroken as she had not really been in love with him, but she missed his company and her pride was somewhat hurt. No-one had since come along to take his place; being stuck at home did not give her much opportunity to meet eligible bachelors. She had asked her father more than once if she could work in the office of his factory but so far he had always found an excuse.

The following day, the ship docked in the Isle of Mull, and the weather was dry and quite warm. Gladys and Eliza had arranged to take a carriage tour of the island, whilst Will and Joss planned to go walking in the countryside, after an initial look round the small town of Tobermory, with its colourful buildings. As they wandered around, Will said:

"I think you were quite taken with Gladys last night, weren't you?"

Joss admitted he was. "It would have been nice if they could have joined us this morning. Perhaps we can all do something together another day."

That evening at dinner, they learned a little more about the Healeys. Eliza and her husband, Henry, had had a younger daughter, Alice, who had married in 1907 and then died shortly after her honeymoon in Paris, as a result of a freak skating accident while there. Eliza had tears in her eyes and her voice cracked more than once as she described the circumstances of her death.

The next day, the ship docked in Skye and they all four explored the town of Portree together in the morning. Once again, they were lucky with the weather. In the afternoon, Gladys accompanied the men on a short walk out into the countryside, while Eliza joined forces with a couple of women of her own age whom she had met the previous day. Gladys asked William and Joss about their parents and their early lives. They told her that their mother had been widowed young and had supported the three of them through her skills as a dressmaker. Will said that he had stayed at school until he was nearly sixteen and then become a junior clerk in the Huddersfield branch of the music shop for which he was now a manager, while Joss had won a scholarship to Oxford University.

"What made you decide to go to Malaya?" Gladys asked Joss.

"Limited options, I suppose," he replied. "To go into many professions, like law or accounting, I would have had to pay a premium, which I did not have, and I would have earned very little in the early years. The colonial civil service was always sold to us at Oxford as an ideal career choice for those graduates without any family money behind them. However, I'm very happy with my choice. I enjoy the life out there, and we all feel that we do a worthwhile job."

That evening, at dinner, Eliza brought up the famous scandal in Malaya which had been in all the English newspapers lately and was about to be the subject of a court case, starting the following week. The wife of a British schoolteacher living in Kuala Lumpur had shot and killed another British man, a neighbour, claiming that he had tried to rape her. However, there were rumours that she was actually having an affair with him. Joss told her that he had met both the men concerned - they were members of the Selangor Club - but did not know either of them well and had no idea of the truth of the matter. The conversation led on to a discussion of what life was like for European women in Malaya.

"In many ways, they have a very easy and pleasant life," Joss said, "especially in Kuala Lumpur and other large towns, where there is a very active social life and the women all support each other. They have few domestic duties as we all have native servants, and the homes we live in are mostly quite spacious. Out in the more remote areas, life can be a bit less amenable, but they are often not there for long at a time. Changes of postings are very frequent and one can find oneself going back and forth from the main towns to the outer districts. I have lived in several places over the last seven years."

Eliza asked about sanitation and other amenities, and he described the usual style of bathroom, on the lower ground floor of the houses, which were built on stilts with a veranda.

"It has a concrete floor with a drainage hole in the corner - with mesh over it to prevent snakes getting in! - and there's an enormous earthenware receptacle which we call a Shanghai jar, or sometimes a Siam jar, which is kept full of cold water, and you simply ladle the water over yourself, using a very large wooden scoop. It's actually a very refreshing way of washing in such a hot climate - you wouldn't want to take a typical English hot bath! However, I'm afraid that the lavatory is often rather like an outside privy; we call it a thunderbox!"

The next day, they docked in Uist, described in the guide book as a paradise for walkers. The weather still being good, Will and Joss set off on a full day's hike. Gladys would have liked to go with them, but knew that her long skirt would probably impede their progress and in any case Eliza would have disapproved of her spending the whole day in remote countryside with two young men.

The following evening, after another warm, dry day spent on the Isle of Harris, there was Scottish dancing on board the boat. Joss thought Gladys looked particularly beautiful in a elegant turquoise evening dress, with a slim layered skirt, short sleeves and low neck. Her hair was piled high and wide on her head, but the style somehow managed to survive the frequent twirling and jigging of the Scottish reels. After engaging in several very energetic dances, Joss and Gladys were feeling quite hot and told the others that they would go up on deck to cool off.

"Take your wrap," Eliza said to Gladys "or you'll catch your death."

Up on deck they leaned over the rail and watched the waves as the ship sailed towards their next - and last - port of call, the Isle of Lewis.

"In less than two days, this trip will be over," Gladys said regretfully.

"It's been a wonderful holiday, and especially because of meeting you," Joss replied, "but the end of the cruise doesn't need to mean the end of our friendship, does it? Brighouse is not far from Heckmondwike and I'll be there until October."

Gladys' heart gave a little leap of joy, and she happily agreed that they could continue to meet. She pushed from her mind the thought of the inevitable parting in October and resolved just to focus on the pleasures of the next few months.

The night before they docked at Oban, Eliza invited the two men to tea on the following Sunday.

"Bring your wife and the children," she said to Will, "and you can all meet the rest of our family."

As they said their farewells on the dock the next morning, Joss ventured to kiss Gladys on the cheek. Eliza raised her eyebrows, but made no comment.

On the train on the way home, Will asked, " Have you thought ahead to October, when you will have to say goodbye to her?"

"Of course I have."

"Wouldn't it be better not to get too close to her in the next few months, for both your sakes?"

"Maybe, but maybe not. Perhaps I'll decide I want to marry her and she might feel the same way. I'm just going to continue seeing her and let things take their natural course."

"I can't see Eliza being very happy about her going to live in Malaya, especially in view of what happened to her sister."

"You're probably right, but she's a grown woman and will be able to make her own choices."

Will looked sceptical but dropped the subject.

~ * ~

Chapter 2

The following Sunday afternoon, the whole family made their way to Brighouse. As they walked from the station along the Huddersfield Road, Theresa pushed Leslie in his chair, Will gave Mabel a piggy-back and Donald walked side by side with Joss.

"How far is it?" he asked.

"Not far now," Joss replied. " I'm looking out for the numbers."

It was quite a large house, set back from the road and at a higher level, with the front garden sloping down to a wall, into which a gate was inset.

"They're obviously better off than us," Theresa observed.

"Well, he owns a factory," Will said. "He's a wire manufacturer."

The door was opened by a young woman in a maid's uniform. As they entered, Gladys came out into the hall, smiling.

"I'm so glad you could all make it; please come through."

In the front parlour, she introduced them to her father, Henry, her brother, Frank - who was a year or two older than she - and her cousin William Stocks, a little younger.

"Mother will be with us in a moment; she's just helping Mary Ellen with the tea."

They settled themselves into chairs and Theresa lifted Leslie into her lap, after telling the other children to sit nicely and be quiet. Eliza came in and was introduced to Theresa and the children. She started to chat to Theresa while Henry and Frank engaged Will in conversation.

" Why don't I take these two young men and this little lady out into the garden where they can play?" Will Stocks suggested. "Until tea's ready."

Theresa gratefully agreed and he shepherded them out of the room.

After half an hour or so, the maid came in with the tea trolley. There was a variety of sandwiches, pastries and cakes and everything was served on delicate china. Luckily, a high chair and unbreakable crockery had been found for Leslie, but Theresa kept a nervous eye on Donald and Mabel in case they broke or spilt anything.

Eliza glanced over to the far corner of the room where Joss and Gladys were talking quietly to each other and Theresa followed her gaze.

"It seems that my daughter and your brother-in-law have struck up quite a friendship," she said. "He's a very nice young man and normally I'd be happy to welcome him as a suitor for Gladys, but he's returning to Malaya in a few months so there can be no future in it."

Theresa was unsure how best to respond to this, but luckily Leslie chose that moment to demand her attention and she was saved from replying.

By the time they left, a return invitation had been issued for three weeks ahead and Joss had arranged to see Gladys the following afternoon.

During the course of the next few weeks, Joss and Gladys met as often as they could. Being on leave, Joss had few commitments and Gladys could usually engineer it so that she finished her chores by midday. The weather had become more unsettled for a week or two after their return from the cruise, but then became dry and quite hot from the end of June. They did not know it then, but this was the beginning of the 1911 heat wave which was to last until September. They took walks out into the countryside, went to a Saturday evening dance, and took Mabel to the park on several occasions; there they could sit and talk while she played on the swings and slide. They found that they had a great deal in common, particularly with regard to their tastes in literature and music.

One afternoon in the park, as they watched Mabel playing happily - Joss having just finished pushing her high on the swing - Gladys asked him whether he would like children of his own.

"Yes, I would. And you?"

"Yes, of course."

He ventured to ask her whether she had ever come close to marrying and she told him about her aborted romance.

"He must have been out of his mind to prefer someone else to you!" Joss exclaimed. "You are beautiful, intelligent and a lovely person."

She blushed. "Well, I'm glad that *you* think so."

He took her hand, leaned towards her, and kissed her gently on the lips. She responded, hesitantly at first then with increasing passion. When they eventually broke apart, he said simply:

"I have fallen in love with you."

" And I with you, " she responded, throwing her arms around him again.

They sat for a while, cuddled together, revelling in the joy of the moment, until they were interrupted by Mabel running over to them.

The return invitation to tea at Cambridge street necessitated the front room being turned back into a parlour, with Joss' bed being remade into a settee. As he and Will wrestled with the intricacies of the various metal parts, Will asked how things were progressing with Gladys. Joss told him that they had declared their feelings for each other.

"Has she told her parents that?" Will asked.

"Not as far as I know. Before I return to Malaya, I intend to ask her to marry me and, assuming she accepts, I suppose I will have to formally speak to her father and ask him for her hand in marriage."

"Good luck with that!" Will said drily.

Theresa had been busy baking for several days and the tea party went off very well. However, as they cleared up afterwards, she remarked that it had been a lot of work and she hoped that such entertaining was not going to become a habit!

Shortly after that, Donald's school term ended, and Joss and Gladys took the two older children to Blackpool for the day. Gladys joined the train at Brighouse which the others had already boarded further down the line; Joss leaning out of the window to indicate the carriage they were in. She ran up the platform, holding a large picnic basket in one hand, which Mary Ellen had packed for them. They all needed to run to catch their connecting train in Manchester, and collapsed laughing into a carriage just as the train pulled out.

In Blackpool, they walked along the promenade, and explored one of the piers, trying out the amusements. Mabel liked the penny slot machines, but Donald preferred the rides. On the beach, the adults sat in deckchairs, side by side so that they could hold hands, while the children took donkey rides, and then they all watched a Punch & Judy show, laughing out loud at the antics of the puppets. After they had eaten their picnic, Donald and Mabel built a sandcastle, having brought their buckets and spades. Gladys looked enviously at the bathing machine, and wished that she had brought her swimming costume.

"We could have a paddle, at least," Joss said, and they all went into the sea, Joss with his trousers rolled up and Gladys with her skirt hitched up to her knees. She rather wished she could tuck it into her drawers, as she had just done with Mabel's, but that would not have been very ladylike. Joss ventured to admire her shapely legs and she smiled and leaned forward to kiss him, nearly overbalancing as a wave caught her, much to the children's amusement. Joss grabbed her just in time, and, laughing, they all made their way back to the beach.

Now that Donald was on holiday from school, he accompanied them on trips to the park, which meant that he and Mabel largely amused themselves, leaving Joss and Gladys free to concentrate on each other, provided they kept the children within sight and hearing.

They walked along the paths and sat on the benches, talking, kissing, laughing. They shared a lot of their innermost thoughts and feelings, although Joss as yet made no mention of marriage. He was partly awaiting the right moment and partly putting off the probable showdown with her parents, who would almost certainly not be keen on her coming to Malaya. However, if he left it too late, it would not be possible for them to be married before he left and for her to return with him or on the next available ship. In that case, they would either have to wait for his next leave - which would be at least five years - or they would have to be married in Malaya, without their families present.

Gladys, for her part, was hoping he would soon propose, but she was also quite fearful of her parents' reactions and did not want anything to spoil their happiness. Whenever she was with him, she felt euphoric; all her senses were on high alert, and everything seemed wonderful. She was quite surprised that Henry and Eliza were allowing her to spend so much time with him, sometimes alone, without commenting on it or questioning her about her feelings. However, her parents were not in fact totally ignoring the situation and had discussed it between them.

"What are we going to do if he proposes and wants to take her to Malaya?" Eliza asked her husband anxiously.

"Well, I don't see that we can stand in her way," Henry replied. "She's thirty-two years old and no-one has so far proposed to her! He's a nice young man, from a decent family - his brother is well thought of amongst the Heckmondwike traders - and he has good prospects out there; he can support a wife."

"But Malaya! It's so far away and they only come home on leave every five years or so. We've lost one daughter; this would be almost like losing the other!"

"Well, let's cross that bridge when we come to it, if we do."

In late August, Joss and Gladys went to Hardcastle Craggs for the day, a famous local beauty spot. They took the train to the small mill town of Hebden Bridge and found that a bus went up the hill to the point where the road to the Craggs branched off. It was a fairly short walk from there to the tiny hamlet of Midgehole, from where a path led into the woods. It was another very hot day, but as it was a weekday there were not too many other day trippers around. They wandered along by the side of the river, and crossed the stepping stones - Gladys holding up her skirt in order to straddle the gaps - then walked along the other side, up to the old Gibson Mill. This was a former cotton mill which had closed in 1890 and since become a leisure centre for the many visitors to the Craggs. There was a cafe and they ordered a late lunch. As they ate, Gladys said:

" I wish this day would never end! Whenever I'm with you, I feel so tremendously happy; the world seems a perfect place where nothing can go wrong, but when we're apart, I can't stop myself thinking ahead and wondering how I 'm going to bear it after you have returned to Malaya!"

Joss studied her for a long moment. Now was the time. He glanced around and saw that they were presently alone in the room.

"You could come with me, or, at any rate, follow as soon as possible. I should go down on one knee for this, shouldn't I?"

He stood up, pushed back his chair and went to Gladys' side. He knelt and took her hand.

"Gladys, my darling, I love you more than I ever thought was possible and I can't bear to be without you either. Would you do me the honour of becoming my wife?"

"Yes, oh yes! " she said, with a little gasp, and flung her arms around him.

The cafe staff, who had come in as he was kneeling and had watched the proceedings from the far end of the room, burst into applause. The waitress came over to them.

"It's a pity we don't have any champagne to offer you, but you can have a pot of tea on the house!"

They laughed and accepted.

As they walked slowly back through the woods, they talked about their future life together in the country Joss had come to love, and which Gladys was eager to experience. They also made plans to go and buy a ring the next day.

"There's a nice jewellers' in Heckmondwike, near your brother's shop," Gladys said. "I'll come over to you as soon as I can tomorrow, shall I?"

"I should first speak to your father," Joss said, "and formally ask for your hand in marriage."

"I suppose so. I'm not sure how he and mother will take it - especially mother. She won't want me to go so far away, particularly in view of what happened to Alice. After Alice died, she had what you might call a complete breakdown - we feared for her sanity at one point."

As they arrived outside the Healeys' home, Henry was just approaching from the other direction.

"Hello, you two! It's been another scorcher of a day, hasn't it? Was it cooler in the woods?"

They exchanged small talk as they walked up the path. As they entered the house, Gladys said:

"Father, Joss wants to speak with you - in private."

"Yes, of course. We'll go in the front room. Gladys, you'd better go and help your mother and Mary Ellen and tell them there'll be another for tea - you will stay Joss, won't you?"

As they sat down, Joss took a deep breath and came straight to the point.

"Sir, I love your daughter very much and I'm therefore asking you for her hand in marriage."

Henry smiled, unsurprised. "And I suppose you've already asked her and she's said yes?"

"Yes, sir."

"Do stop calling me sir! Of course I give you both my blessing. However, there are some provisos. Am I right in thinking that you'll be planning to marry in the next few weeks and take her back with you to Malaya?"

"Well, we do hope to marry before I return, so that our families can be present, but it may be too short notice to get Gladys a passage on the same ship; she may have to follow later."

"The trouble is, Eliza will take some time to come to terms with this news. To be quite frank with you, she's been rather dreading this happening because she can't bear the thought of Gladys living so far away and seeing her so seldom. I don't want that either, but if it has to be, I won't stand in the way of her happiness. However, is there no chance of you being able to return to England to work here - in London maybe?"

Joss shook his head. "The career progression is very different. I would have to spend a much longer time in Malaya before I would have a chance of getting a half-decent post in England. If I were to just leave now, after only one tour of service, I would have to start on the bottom rung of another career here and I would earn a pittance - barely enough to support myself, let alone a wife. Out there, I will return to a senior position and we will live in a nice, spacious house with several servants. Gladys will have a good life." He then added, "I also love the country and have no desire to leave and Gladys is perfectly happy to share that life with me."

"I understand," Henry said, "but my wife is going to take some convincing. I'm also quite worried about how she will react. After our other daughter died, she had a complete breakdown and took some time to recover. I don't want to trigger that again - we need to tread carefully and give her time to get used to the idea, so Gladys may not be able to follow you straight away. Anyway, let's go and talk to her - there's no point in putting it off!"

They went into the back room, where Eliza, Gladys and Mary Ellen were engaged in laying out the meal. It was a large kitchen cum living room, with a substantial cooking range, and there was a door leading through to a good sized scullery and larder.

"Well, Father," Gladys said, on tenterhooks. "What did you say?"

"I gave you both my blessing, in principle," Henry said, smiling.

Gladys gave a squeal of joy. "Thank you!"

"However, exactly when you marry and when you go to Malaya has still to be discussed with your mother," he warned.

Eliza had stopped what she was doing to listen to this exchange. She rounded on her husband.

"Didn't you think to speak to me first, before giving your consent?"

"No. It's customary for the bride's father to be asked and to give consent. You know that."

"And you know how I feel about her going so far away - and I'm surprised that you're so calm about it! She's your only living daughter - do you want to not see her for years on end?"

"Of course not, but we can't stand in the way of their happiness. They love each other, Eliza. It's unfortunate his work is so far away, but we will have to accept the situation. Now, we have to discuss when and where they get married and when Gladys follows him out there."

"We have enough time to fit the wedding in before Joss leaves," Gladys said eagerly. "He doesn't sail until 19th October."

"Well, apart from anything else, that's not enough time," Eliza said. "Do you have any idea how long it takes to arrange a wedding? I was planning Alice's for nearly a year."

"It doesn't need to take that long. We don't want a large fancy wedding, do we Joss? Just a small simple ceremony with our immediate families and a few close friends will be fine."

"If you have such a meagre rushed wedding, people will wonder whether you are expecting!"

"Perhaps it's a pity that I'm not - at least that would instil a sense of urgency in you! If we don't marry before Joss leaves, then we'll have to have the wedding in Malaya and neither of our families will be present. Is that what you want?!"

"That's out of the question! You'll have to wait until he next comes home on leave. You've only known each other a couple of months; it's not nearly long enough to be sure of your feelings. On the basis of such a short acquaintance, you're proposing to go and live thousands of miles away in a hot, humid, heathen country, no doubt riddled with deadly tropical diseases.... Anyway, why can't Joss get a job in England?"

"We've gone through that," Henry interjected. "It's not feasible."

"It's not a heathen country!" Gladys exclaimed. "It's ruled by the British. As for the weather, it's probably not much hotter than we've been having here this summer, and I'm no more likely to catch a tropical disease that I am to catch pneumonia during a typical English winter!....... And we can't wait until his next leave - that won't be for another five years at least. We can't be apart that long, and we want to have children - it might be too late for me by then!" Her voice was rising in panic and anger.

"Nonsense, plenty of women have children in their late thirties, and into their forties."

"Not the first one!"

As Gladys and Eliza glared at each other, they were interrupted by the arrival of Frank and Will.

"What's going on?" Frank asked. "I could hear you all before I opened the front door!"

"Gladys and Joss are engaged to be married," Henry answered him, "and we are just discussing the practicalities. They want to be married before Joss leaves in October and for Gladys to follow him as soon as possible, but your mother does not like the idea."

"Well, congratulations, anyway," Frank said, kissing his sister on the cheek and shaking Joss' hand. "I hope you'll both be very happy."

"If Mother has her way, we won't get the chance to be happy," Gladys said, by now near to tears.

Henry decided that was enough for the moment. He turned to Joss.

"Joss, I'm sorry. I know I invited you to stay for tea, but I think it might be better if you left us for now and let us continue this conversation amongst ourselves."

Joss nodded and turned to go. Gladys followed him out of the room and to the door. On the doorstep, he turned and took her in his arms.

"I *will* bring her round," she said, half sobbing, "we can't be made to wait five years!"

"I will wait for you as long as it takes," he said gently, brushing the tears from her cheek with his finger, "but I hope it won't be that long. I'll see you tomorrow, shall I, as we agreed?"

"Yes, I'll be there - whatever happens."

They kissed and held each other tightly, then he turned and set off down the path.

When he reached Brighouse station, he found there were delays with the train service and by the time he got home, his earlier elation had almost totally evaporated. Tea had long since been cleared away and the children were in bed. Will and Theresa looked at him enquiringly.

"You've had your tea, I assume?" Theresa asked.

"No, actually, I haven't."

She started to rise. "Then I'll get you something."

He stopped her with a hand on her shoulder. "No, Theresa, you've probably only just sat down. I'll make myself a sandwich."

"Well, I'll put the kettle on," she replied, reaching across to the range.

After he had eaten, he started to tell them what had transpired. When they heard that he had proposed and been accepted, they interrupted with their congratulations, Theresa kissing him on the cheek and Will shaking him warmly by the hand.

"Wait until you hear the rest of it."

"Did her father refuse consent?" Will asked.

"No, he was fine about it and gave us his blessing - it's her mother who's the problem." He outlined the gist of the argument between Eliza and Gladys.

"So, how was it left?" Will asked.

"Henry said they'd be better off talking about it further between themselves. That's why I left before tea - and then there were train delays, hence I'm so late back."

Theresa and Will were quiet for a while, thinking about the situation, then Theresa said:

"I suppose I can see Eliza's point of view. As the mother of a daughter, I'd be heartbroken if she wanted to go and live so far away."

"So would I," Will said, "but we wouldn't stand in the way of her happiness, would we? Our mother was pretty upset when Joss went out there, but she'd never have tried to stop him."

Joss was silent for a moment, remembering the emotional farewell with his mother on Liverpool dock nearly eight years ago, which turned out to be the last time he would ever see her.

"How old is Gladys?" Theresa asked.

"Thirty-two."

"So she'll be thirty-seven when you come back again. It is cutting it a bit fine for having children, but by no means impossible."

"It's not just the question of children," Joss said. "We love each other far too much to stand being apart for as long as five years, and it might even be a bit longer; five years is now the official period for a second tour of duty but it often runs over that."

"If you do get married in Malaya," Will said thoughtfully, "You could always have your marriage blessed in church here when you come back on leave. Both families can be present at that ceremony and you could have a small reception afterwards."

"That's a good idea," Joss agreed, brightening slightly. "That might just help to convince Eliza."

26

"In any case, I wouldn't be too despondent yet," Theresa said. "Henry seems to be on your side, and probably Frank too, so maybe they will be able to persuade her. Anyway, can't they all just overrule her?"

"I doubt that they will. Henry said she would have to be given time to come to terms with it. Apparently, she had a serious breakdown after Gladys' sister died and they're afraid of that happening again." He sighed and added: " I was the happiest man alive this afternoon, after she accepted me, but now I feel quite gloomy about the future."

~ * ~

Chapter 3

The next day, Gladys arrived fairly early. Joss was in the front room and saw her from the window. He was at the door before she knocked, and saw immediately from her face that there had been no positive resolution the previous night. She put her arms around his neck and laid her cheek against his.

"I'm so sorry, darling. I still can't tell you when I can travel to Malaya and it's looking very unlikely that we can be married before you go."

"What happened after I left?" he asked, as they went through into the back room.

"Very little. Father put a veto on discussing it while we ate our meal, and then afterwards Mother made one excuse after another to avoid sitting down with us. Father eventually insisted that she did, but she was still adamant that it was too soon to be married before you sail and marriage in Malaya was also out of the question! Then she went to bed early. Father, Frank and I continued to talk about it - at least they are both on my side - and Father said I'd better leave it to him to discuss it with her when they are on their own, after she's calmed down a bit, and gradually get her to come round to the idea - if he can!"

Joss relayed to her the suggestion Will had come up with, of having a blessing on their marriage in five years time, assuming they had married in Malaya meanwhile. Her face lit up somewhat.

"Oh, yes! I'll tell Father that and perhaps it will help him to persuade her."

"Just how bad was your mother's breakdown after Alice died?"

"It was really terrible. At first she grieved bitterly, as you would expect and as we all did, but then instead of slowly and gradually recovering, she went into a decline. There were periods when she wouldn't get out of bed and many days when she wouldn't even wash herself; we had to take her to the bathroom and do it for her. The doctor said it was melancholia and not uncommon following bereavement. It was quite frightening at the time; we all felt totally helpless - she wouldn't even talk to any of us. Eventually, she slowly got better and she has been fine now for a couple of years, but I know Father is terrified of a relapse - we all are. God knows, I don't want to make her ill again, but it seems to be our happiness against hers right now!"

He pulled her to him and held her close. "Well it seems that we will have to leave it in your father's hands for now and not try to force the issue. I don't want to be responsible for making your mother ill again either, and you wouldn't be the person I thought you were if you were unconcerned about that."

"Do you still want us to be engaged," Gladys asked anxiously, "or would you rather I released you, under the circumstances?"

"Of course I still want it! I love you and I told you I'd wait for you as long as it takes."

"You say that now, but when you get back to Malaya, you might meet someone else who is free to marry you." Her voice shook.

"Oh, ye of little faith!" he exclaimed. Cupping her face in his hands, he continued: "I've never felt like this about anyone in thirty-one years and I'm not going to be deterred by a few more years delay. There will never be anyone else for me."

"What if it turns out to be too late for us to have children?"

"It probably won't be, but anyway I want you even more than I want children. Even if we don't succeed in having a baby, I want to grow old with you and be with you until death finally parts us!"

Theresa came into the room, along with Mabel and Leslie.

"Are we going to the park?" Mabel asked hopefully.

"Not today, love," Joss answered. "Auntie Gladys and I are going to buy an engagement ring." The children had been told at breakfast that he and Gladys were to be married.

"Was anything resolved last night?" Theresa asked.

Gladys shook her head and gave her a condensed version of events. Then a thought struck her.

"Would you come and talk to her? Later, I mean, after Joss has gone back. You could bring the children over for a visit, and then bring the conversation round to our situation. She might just listen to you; after all, you are also a mother."

Theresa looked doubtful. "Well, I could, and of course I'd like to help, but I doubt I'd get anywhere. I'm your age group, not hers, and my children are still small. It would be better if someone her own age tried to convince her. Do you know of a friend or relative who might be willing to do that?"

Gladys thought for a minute or two. "Oh yes! My aunt - her sister. She lives in London - maybe I could stay with her the night before Joss sails." She turned to him:

"I know you're staying with your friend, but would you be able to come over for part of the evening, so that she can make your acquaintance? Then I'll try to get her on my side. And if I stay the night there, I can come to Tilbury with you the next morning!"

He agreed that that was a good plan, and she said she'd write to her aunt that evening.

On the way to the jewellers, Gladys asked him to let her know his upper price limit.

"Are you being paid while on leave?"

"I'm on half pay now. It was full pay for the first six months. Don't worry, I can afford a nice ring."

However, the ring she eventually chose was one of the less expensive ones they had been shown.

"This one is just what I want, and look, it fits perfectly, so no need to have it altered and I can wear it straight away."

Back at Cambridge Street, they sat in the garden. Gladys asked if he had a recent photograph of himself she could have.

"Afraid you'll forget what I look like?" he teased.

"Of course not, but I'd like to put a framed picture of you on my bedside table - it will make me feel closer to you."

"I'd like one of you too. Actually Will took quite a few photographs on the cruise and there are some of us together - I'm sure he can spare a couple."

After tea, William got out his photograph collection. "There are also still some on the second film, which I've not yet finished."

"Why don't you finish it now then?" Joss suggested, "and take some pictures of us all in the garden - before the children go to bed - and then I can have up to date photographs of everyone."

So they had a photographic session on the lawn and Will said he'd get the film developed the next day. Gladys then rifled through his collection and turned up some much older pictures, below all the ones of the children.

"Are these you two?" she asked.

Will glanced at one of them. "Yes, that's me and Joss when we were about five and three."

She insisted on looking at them all, devouring this vision of her lover's childhood. There was also one of Joss in gown and mortar board on his graduation from Oxford and another of him with his rowing team.

"Am I going to be allowed to see you as a child, too?" Joss asked.

"If you must - I'll dig out the family album when we are next there."

The hot weather continued to hold into early September and they took another day trip, this time to the moors above Haworth. There was a slight breeze here, but it was still too hot to walk far. They found a secluded spot, well away from the path, where an overhanging rock provided some welcome shade. Joss had brought the picnic this time and he had included a thin blanket in his backpack. They spread this out on the grass and sat down to eat. Afterwards, they lay back and started to kiss and caress each other. Both of them had been wearing the minimum of thin summer clothing ever since the heat wave started. Gladys had ditched her corset and just had a thin camisole under her muslin blouse. Joss undid the buttons of the blouse and fondled and kissed her breasts. Soon, they had both divested themselves of most of their clothes, their desire was becoming ever more intense and their lovemaking increasingly intimate.

"We mustn't get too carried away," he said. "We can't risk leaving you with a baby!"

"Maybe that wouldn't be too bad an idea, then Mother would have to let us get married!"

"No, sweetheart, that's not how we should start our life together. It would destroy your reputation and forfeit your father's good opinion of me. But we can still give each other some pleasure...."

Later, they lay drowsily in each other's arms.

"I love you so very much," she said. "How am I going to bear life without you?"

He had no answer for that and just buried his face in her long dark hair, which had come loose from its pins.

On 11th September, the prolonged heat wave came to an abrupt end. The temperature plummeted and the heavens opened. After that there were no more opportunities to be alone in remote areas of the countryside. When the weather was dry enough, they were able to go on some short walks and also take Mabel and Leslie to the park. Otherwise, they had to spend time at each other's homes. Eliza left them alone in the front room for periods, but they felt constrained by her presence in the house, particularly in view of her antipathy to their marriage, and generally preferred to be at Cambridge Street. One day, Theresa took the two younger children to see her family for the day, and asked them to be there when

Donald came home from school, so that she did not have to rush back, which meant that they had the house to themselves until then. They spent much of that time on the bed in the front room, indulging their passion as far as they dared.

September merged into October and they were now acutely aware of just how little time they had left. From then on, they spent every day together, including Sunday mornings; Gladys accompanying the family to Heckmondwike parish church, where William was the relief organist. He was playing on one of those Sundays, and afterwards Gladys complimented him on his performance, prompting Joss to comment:

"Yes, he's come a long way since he used to pound away at his scales on our old piano, while I was trying to concentrate on my homework!"

Gladys sometimes cycled over from Brighouse and, as the nights were drawing in, Joss borrowed Will's bike after tea and accompanied her home. Saying goodnight each evening became increasingly prolonged as neither of them wanted to pull away.

A few days before Joss' departure date, he packed his trunk and arranged for its transportation to Tilbury dock. Later that evening, he and his brother played chess. Will won the first game quickly and easily, which was unusual, and when he also won the second game within a short space of time, he said:

"Either you're letting me win as a goodbye present, or you're just not concentrating!"

Joss smiled ruefully. "You know, if I hadn't met Gladys, or if she was coming with me, I'd be looking forward to returning to Malaya and my job. It's been a marvellous year, and I'll be very sad to leave you all, but I've been a gentleman of leisure for long enough and I'm ready to get back to work. However, as things are, I feel completely torn in two."

Will said thoughtfully: "I know you can't imagine it right now, but it will probably be easier than you think once you are back there.

You'll become absorbed in your work, you'll be posted to a new place and you'll have plenty of distractions. I'm not saying you won't be missing her and longing for her to come to you, but it will be bearable."

The morning of the 18th finally dawned. The first goodbyes were with Donald and Will before they left for school and work. Joss hugged the little boy, promising to send him picture postcards from Malaya, then turned to his brother. They embraced each other.

"Thanks for everything, Will, and for letting me be a part of your family this past year. I'm going to really miss you all."

"You *are* part of my family," Will said huskily. "Always have been and always will be. And I will miss you too - I've got used to you being around again. Look after yourself out there and come back to us safely next time."

Joss went to the door with them and stood at the gate until they reached the end of the street, where they turned and waved. Blinking hard, he went back into the house. Mabel looked up at him, with a woebegone expression.

"I don't want you to go, Uncle Joss. Why can't you stay here forever?"

"That's not possible," Theresa said gently. "Don't send him off with tears - let his last sight of you be with a happy face!"

Joss lifted her up and she put her arms around his neck. He kissed her and told her she was his favourite niece.

"I'm your *only* niece!"

"Ah, well, you may not always be the only one, but you'll still be my favourite!"

He then picked Leslie up and swung him overhead until he squealed in delight.

"Well, little fellow, you won't remember me when I come again, but I shan't forget you!"

Gladys arrived on time, carrying her overnight bag. He turned to his sister-in-law.

"Thanks, Theresa, for looking after me so well. I shall miss you and I'll be missing your wonderful cooking for a long time to come!"

"Get on with you!" she exclaimed, blushing at the compliment. "We'll all miss you too - we've enjoyed having you here."

He kissed her on both cheeks, gave Mabel one final hug, then put on his hat and coat and picked up his case. Theresa followed them out to the gate, Leslie in her arms and Mabel by her side, and he too turned at the end of the street and waved.

On the journey to London, the train was full and they made little conversation, just sitting close together and holding hands tightly. After seeing Gladys to her aunt Lavinia's house in Bloomsbury, Joss went over to his friend's home, which was not far away, for a couple of hours. He had last seen Leonard in April but, as that was before he had met Gladys, they had a lot of catching up to do.

He arrived back at Lavinia's in good time for dinner. She was the widow of a wealthy man and lived in a large town house with several servants. Over the meal they discussed their predicament and she appeared to be sympathetic. She asked Joss several searching questions about his background and about life in Malaya, and he hoped he had managed to give a good impression of both. As he left, Gladys followed him to the door. After they kissed goodnight, she said:

"Aunt Lavinia liked you - I could tell. She'll be on our side."

The next morning, they took the boat train to Tilbury. Again, it was crowded and there was little opportunity for private conversation. They sat close together, each with a tight knot of misery churning inside them. At the docks, Joss had to first locate his trunk and arrange for its loading onto the ship, then they had only a short time left before embarkation. The tears Gladys had been holding back started to overflow.

"I wasn't going to do this!" she sobbed. "I planned to send you off with a smile so that would be your last memory of me, but I can't, I just can't!"

"I can't either!" Joss said thickly, the lump in his throat threatening to choke him.

They clung to each other desperately, their bodies pressed tightly together. As the queue started to form for boarding, he covered her face with kisses, their tears mingling.

"Don't go! Please don't go!" she cried, the last vestiges of self control deserting her.

"I have to! You know I do."

After one last fierce hug, he prised himself from her and headed for the gangway.

"I'll stay here until you sail," she called after him.

"I'll wave from the deck!"

Wiping his hand across his eyes, he went up the steps and disappeared inside the ship. After depositing his case in his allocated cabin, he raced up on deck, and leaned over the rail. She was still there, waiting anxiously for him to appear. They waved to each other, blowing kisses and mouthing words of love.

As the ship pulled away from the dock, the crowd around her started to disperse, but she remained where she stood and he remained on deck. They both stayed rooted to the spot, the expanse of sea lengthening between them, until each was a mere speck on the horizon.

End of Part I

Part II

Chapter 4

Joss docked in Penang at the end of November. After a few days in Kuala Lumpur, he was posted to Kuala Kubu, some 25 miles north, as Assistant District Officer. This was a temporary position, until a more senior one became available. The small town had been partly destroyed by a flood from a burst dam in 1883 and planned rebuilding work had not yet commenced, so it was in rather a sorry state with a lot of derelict buildings.

The first few weeks in his new job were particularly busy, as he familiarised himself with the district, and he had to admit that his brother had been right about there being plenty of distractions to prevent him brooding about Gladys, at least during the working day. It was in the late evening, alone in his bungalow, that he craved her presence. He regularly fantasised about how it would be if she were with him: coming home to her after a hard day's work, discussing the day's events over dinner and retiring to bed together.

Shortly before Christmas, he opened the cards he had been given in England before he sailed and put them on display. The three children had all made their own cards for him. He was not sure what Leslie's drawing was meant to be, but the other two were recognisably a robin and a Christmas tree. They made him feel quite nostalgic, as did Will and Theresa's card with its traditional snow covered scene. The one from Gladys, with its words of love, stabbed at his heart. On Christmas morning, he opened their presents: Gladys had given him some beautiful cufflinks which looked quite expensive. He would wear them for dances at the Selangor Club when he was next in Kuala Lumpur, he thought. Maybe she would even be with him by then?

He spent the rest of Christmas day with Reg, the D.O. whom he assisted, and Dorothy, his buxom, good-natured wife. Reg was a genial, florid faced fellow in his fifties, not far off retirement. The day passed very pleasantly, but he could not help contrasting it with the large, jolly family gathering of the previous year.

He wrote to Gladys each week, as well as to Will every few weeks, as he had always done. In his letters to Gladys, he described his day to day activities, painting a picture for her of the life she would eventually share with him, emphasising, however, that he was presently in a rural area with a limited social life.

Gladys' first letter had reached him only a week or so after landing. She had sent it while still staying at her aunt's in London. She told him that Lavinia had written to Eliza, inviting herself to stay for Christmas and the New Year, which would give them plenty of time and opportunity for private conversation.

~ * ~

After leaving the dock, Gladys had cried all the way back to London on the train. She had made no sound but had been quite unable to halt the tears pouring down her face. At one point, an elderly lady, sitting opposite, leaned forward, tapped her hand and asked if there was anything she could do. Gladys just shook her head, unable to speak. When she arrived back at her aunt's home, Lavinia took one look at her tear drenched state and promptly sent off a telegram to Henry and Eliza, advising that Gladys would be staying a few more days with her.

"It's probably better if you don't return home until you are calmer; you'd only have a monumental row with your mother and that wouldn't help matters."

When she eventually arrived back home, she had to bite her tongue to prevent herself expressing her anger at Eliza. At that point in time, she almost hated her mother; if it were not for her, she and Joss would be married and she would be following him out there on the next available ship. However, she had promised her aunt that she would not provoke an argument prior to Lavinia's visit. So she was calm and civil in her dealings with her mother, but there was none of the easy friendship there had previously been between them. Eliza, for her part, mourned the loss of her close relationship with her daughter and spoke about it to Henry:

"Well, are you surprised? You've caused her to be separated from the love of her life - you can hardly expect her to be happy about it!"

"I'm not just being selfish. Whilst it's true I can't bear to think of her so far away and seeing her so seldom, I'm also seriously concerned about her welfare. You don't seem to have given that much consideration. She'll be thousands of miles away from everyone and everything she knows, and if it doesn't work out too well with Joss, after the honeymoon period is over, she could be desperately unhappy."

"All marriages are a gamble, to a certain extent," Henry replied, "but when a couple love each other, they can usually work things out. It's not as if they are too young to know their own minds - they are both in their thirties."

"There's also the question of her physical health," Eliza continued. "Especially if she conceives a child when they are in one of those remote districts. The nearest medical facilities could be many hours' journey away. If there are complications.....it doesn't bear thinking about! And then there's the climate; it takes a lot of adjusting to, I believe, and can be very debilitating, especially for women."

"Well, as far as childbirth is concerned, I daresay Joss could arrange for her to stay in Kuala Lumpur, where the European hospital is, when her time is near."

"But what if there are complications earlier on?"

"You seem to be looking for problems, Eliza. English women do live out there and bear children. You can't cater for every eventuality. I think we can trust Joss to look after her and have her best interests at heart."

Over the Christmas and New Year period, Lavinia had several heart to heart discussions with Eliza. She acknowledged her concerns, but pointed out that young people had to be allowed to live their own lives and make their own decisions.

"I know you want to wrap her in cotton wool and keep her safe. And it's understandable, after what happened to Alice. But if you continue to prevent her from being with the man she loves, she'll come to hate you for it. Is that what you want?"

"Of course not. I know I'll have to let her go eventually - I've already said she can marry him in five years time when he's next back on leave and return with him. By then, their feelings will have stood the test of time."

"Time spent apart is not necessarily a good test. And five years is a very long time, especially for a woman of Gladys' age, assuming they want children. Why don't you tell her she can go in a couple of years, after she's taken some courses at the School of Oriental Studies in London? She can stay with me while she does them. I believe they have various short courses during the holiday periods. They include learning a smattering of Malay which will stand her in good stead when she gets there. She can also read some books on the country, rather than just relying on what Joss tells her - he may well be leaving out the negative aspects. Making sure she is well prepared before she goes; that is surely the best way to protect her? There's also the question of getting the right wardrobe together for the tropics. There are some specialist shops in London and you could also get your dressmaker to run her up some more thin cotton dresses and so on, nearer the time."

This gave Eliza some food for thought and she said she'd discuss it all with Gladys after Lavinia returned home. It was time they got things out in the open again and stopped skirting around the issue.

She was as good as her word and in January Gladys wrote to Joss and told him the gist of it.

" ....*So it looks like it will only be about two years, darling, not five. And maybe I can bring it forward further, if I get on well with these courses. (After all, you didn't spend two years preparing for Malaya, did you?). Please wait for me - don't be tempted by anyone else you meet out there, will you? I can't help worrying about that, as well as missing you dreadfully. I positively ache for you!"*

Joss replied that it was a good idea to use their enforced time apart to be better prepared for life in Malaya.

"*.....It will make it easier for you to adjust, especially learning some of the language. But don't imagine they'll tell you everything - unless things have changed in the last decade. We were all still quite green when we arrived here...........I'm very glad that we don't have to wait five years, as I am missing you more than words can describe!"*

~ * ~

In March, Joss was transferred to Taiping to be State Treasurer for Perak. Before he left, Dorothy asked him how things were progressing with regard to his fiancee sailing to join him.

"It looks like it will be another couple of years." He relayed the gist of Eliza's concerns and the plan for Gladys to learn more about the country.

"I'm a bit wary of Eliza finding some further excuse later on," he added, "although I may be doing her an injustice."

41

"Well, if it would help, I'll be going to England in time for next Christmas to see my son and daughter and I'll be staying into the New Year. I have a sister in Harrogate, whom I plan to visit, and as Harrogate is not far from your area, I could also pay a visit to Gladys and her mother and tell them first-hand about life here from a woman's point of view. After all, I've been here over twenty years and had two children."

Joss thanked her and said that would be very helpful. He gave her the address before he left.

In Taiping, he was based at the large, imposing government offices, and found a place in a shared bungalow with two colleagues. The town nestled by a lake, surrounded by hills, and their bungalow had a large jacaranda tree in the garden. They employed a houseboy each and shared the cook and the other servants. The reduced living costs meant he could put something away towards his wedding and future married life.

Being a state capital, there were many more Europeans here than in Kuala Kubu and there was a large social club. Joss appreciated being able to drop in there after work and have one or two *Stengahs* (whisky sodas) at the bar with his colleagues. There were also plenty of sporting activities and dances at weekends, and it all served to distract him from missing Gladys. In his letters to her, he described it all in detail, emphasising the activities he thought she would enjoy the most.

~ * ~

Gladys attended her first two week course in London over the Easter period. She enjoyed the lessons and found that the Malayan language was not as difficult to learn as she had feared. In the evenings and over the Easter weekend, she went to the theatre and concerts with Lavinia and accompanied her to one or two dinner parties. At one of these there were a couple of unattached men, one in his thirties and one probably early forties, who both paid her a great deal of attention. She rather enjoyed this, but neither of them attracted her - her heart was totally committed to Joss.

In agreeing to Lavinia's proposals, Eliza had had at the back of her mind the hope that either Gladys would be put off Malaya, after learning about the rigours of life there, or that she would meet someone else while in London. When she returned at the end of the course without either of those things having happened, she was disappointed, but told herself it was early days yet.

When news broke of the sinking of the Titanic on 15th April, a day or two after Gladys' return, Eliza had yet another fear to add to her list - perhaps the ship taking her daughter to Malaya would be sunk! Henry pointed out with some asperity that a ship en route for the South China Seas would be highly unlikely to strike an iceberg, but that did not stop her dwelling on other causes of ships capsizing.

"Don't worry," Henry said privately to Gladys. "She'll soon forget about that one, provided no further such catastrophes are reported in the news!"

William and Theresa's fourth child and third son was born on 1st August 1912. News of this happy event, with accompanying photo of the baby, reached Joss a few weeks later. They named him William Ewart, to be called Ewart. Joss was happy for them, but could not help wondering just how long it would be before he became a father.

Dorothy visited the Healeys as promised in early 1913 and talked at length to Gladys and Eliza about life in Malaya. She told them that life for women was now very much improved, compared to when she first went out there in the early 1890s. They both asked her a lot of questions, Eliza raising all her concerns, and she did her best to answer honestly, but at the same time emphasising the good aspects and making light of the bad ones. Eliza was not entirely convinced that life there was quite as easy as she was portraying it, suspecting that Joss had asked her to paint a rosy picture, but Gladys' enthusiasm for the country was undiminished after her visit.

~ * ~

Joss' posting to Taiping ended in May 1913 and he was transferred to Kuala Lumpur as State Treasurer for Selangor, as well as Assistant Treasurer for the FMS and First Class Magistrate for Selangor. After an initial stay in the cadets' mess, he again shared a bungalow, this time with only one other bachelor. The demands of the new posts were high and at first he was exceptionally busy, resulting in his next letter to Gladys being somewhat delayed. This rather alarmed her until his letter finally arrived, explaining the reason. He assured her that he loved her as much as ever and was just living for the day she would finally join him and they could be married.

"....Only another year, my love, until we can be together. We've survived over eighteen months so far and it has seemed an eternity, but now there is light at the end of the tunnel"......

However, now that he was back in Kuala Lumpur, Joss was tempted to visit the house of ill repute which he had frequented in the past. He ascertained that his favourite Japanese girl was still there and eventually gave in to his baser instincts. She seemed glad to see him again. When he told her he was now engaged and felt guilty that he was betraying his fiancee, she said simply:

"But she's not here, is she? And you are not being unfaithful in your heart."

These Japanese girls were given regular medical examinations under a Government programme and received certificates confirming they were free of disease, so Joss did not think he was risking contracting anything which he might later pass on to Gladys. However, he could not entirely justify his actions to himself, and kept his visits few and far between.

~ * ~

During the summer holiday period of 1913, Gladys attended her fourth course in London. Her grasp of the Malayan language had improved greatly and she had learned quite a lot about the country she was determined to live in. None of it had put her off; not even the insects and reptiles - in fact she quite liked the idea of being cocooned in bed with Joss under a mosquito net.

~ * ~

In December Joss was transferred yet again, this time to be a magistrate in Seremban, state capital of Negri Sembilan, as well as Assistant Superintendent of Immigrants and Deputy Controller of Labour. He was based at the government offices, again shared a bungalow - this time with someone he already knew well - and enjoyed the social life at the club. However, he was only there a few months, and after a very brief spell back in Kuala Lumpur, he was posted to Klang, in early May 1914, to be District Officer and Magistrate, a post which was likely to last at least a year.

Klang was a small town in Selangor State, not too far from Kuala Lumpur. Until 1880 it had been the state capital. There were a fair number of Europeans in the district and there was an active social club. His District Officer's house was a large one and would be a fitting home for he and Gladys to start their married life. There was also a nice church where they could be married. He was expecting any day now to hear what sailing she was booked on; application had been made to the Colonial Office.

However, when the booking for her sea passage finally arrived, it was not until early September. Demand was high at present, apparently, and priority was given to those sailing to work out in the Colonies as well as those returning from leave. Ladies sailing to join their men appeared to be at the bottom of the list. Disappointed, she relayed the news to Joss:

"... Yet more delay before we can be together; if only we'd booked a passage much earlier! But at least we now know exactly when I'll be arriving and you can make arrangements for our wedding..."

Joss went ahead and booked the church for a week after her arrival in October. He reserved a room at the club for a small reception and sent off invitations to a select group of friends, also asking one of them to be his best man. He did not want to invite a lot of people and overwhelm Gladys, who would have none of her own friends and family there. He invited Reg and Dorothy and asked Dorothy to be Gladys' matron of honour. He also arranged for her to stay with a planter couple, from a nearby estate, prior to the wedding. When he relayed this to Gladys she was happy with it all but asked him to also invite a couple of women whom she had met on her courses and who were now in Malaya. He did as she asked and, arrangements now made, relaxed and enjoyed anticipating their life together, now finally within reach.

Then, on 28th June, news broke that the Arch Duke Ferdinand, heir to the Austro-Hungarian empire, had been shot dead in Sarajevo. This was followed by increasingly alarming news bulletins as the western world tried to deal with the repercussions of this act. At the end of July, Austro-Hungary went to war with Serbia, backed by Germany, and Russia prepared for war against both of them. At the beginning of August, Germany declared war on Russia, then France, and finally Britain issued an ultimatum to Germany and declared war on 4th August.

Gladys, in the midst of her preparations for travel, did not at first think that this would delay her departure. However, less than two weeks prior to her sailing date, her ship was commandeered by the war office for use as a troop carrier. In vain she awaited a replacement booking. Henry contacted the colonial office who told him that many more ships were being requisitioned, for use as hospital ships as well as troop carriers and supply vessels. As the remaining ships would be needed to transport essential personnel to the colonies, as well as for mail and freight, women sailing to join their men were the lowest priority. They would put her on a waiting list but were not optimistic that she would be able to sail before the war was over. They also advised against non-essential travel because of the danger to shipping from warfare.

The prevailing view amongst many was that the war would probably be all over in six months or so, but Gladys was still bitterly disappointed. She sent a telegram to Joss advising him of the situation. He approached the colonial office himself, via the High Commissioner of the FMS, but the answer was the same.

With a heavy heart he cancelled all the arrangements he had made. If only she had sailed earlier! This was all Eliza's fault, he thought, and, in a rare display of anger and frustration, he picked up a vase and hurled it against the wall, where it shattered.

~ * ~

Gladys also vented her feelings on her mother, blaming her for everything.

"If only we'd married before Joss left and I'd followed him out there a few months later - as we wanted - we'd have a child by now. But if this war goes on for years, I'll be barren by the time I can sail out there, and God knows when he'll be able to come back on leave. Meanwhile, he'll probably meet someone else and break off our engagement. Thanks for ruining my life, Mother!"

"I still don't think it would have been right to have rushed into marriage," Eliza replied. "I accept that you could perhaps have gone last year, but no-one really thought that we would declare war. You can't blame me for that!"

"I *do* blame you - in fact right now I hate you!" She burst into tears, just as Henry came into the room, and turned on him too.

47

" And you're not much better than her! You professed to be on my side, but you did nothing. You just let her cause delay after delay. Why didn't you book the passage before Christmas at least, when I asked you to? I'd have got there in time then."

Without waiting for a reply, she dashed out of the room and out of the house, tears streaming down her face. She ran headlong into Frank who was coming up the path. He put his hands on her shoulders to stop her flight.

"Hey, Glad, you can't go out into the street in that state!"

"Well, I'm not going back in there, to them. I hate them both - they've ruined everything!"

"I take it there's no hope of a passage, then?"

"Not until the war ends, when I'll probably be an old woman!"

He steered her round into the garden, where they sat on a bench as she let out her misery and frustration. Eventually, he proffered her his hanky, and she mopped her face.

"Well, you can't stay out here forever; we'd better go inside," he said.

She acquiesced, past caring, but went straight up to her bedroom.

"I suggest the two of you at least apologise to her," Frank told his parents. "She's right in that, if it weren't for you, she'd be in Malaya by now and happily married. You can't deny that this situation is at least partly your fault. I think you should beg her forgiveness!"

When Gladys eventually came downstairs, they did as their son had suggested. She reluctantly accepted their apologies, for the sake of peaceful living, but resolved to get out of this house as soon as she could, and, if the war dragged on, get a job for the duration and live elsewhere.

~ * ~

Chapter 5

Meanwhile, in Klang, Joss' houseboy came in to sweep up the broken vase, tiptoeing round his *Tuan* (boss) who still had a face like thunder. He and the other servants were aware of the situation and a week or so later, after he had served dinner, he asked Joss, in Malay, if he could make a suggestion.

"Go ahead."

"The cook has a niece, a nice girl, who's been widowed young. She was married only a few months and there are no children. She's still only eighteen and quite pretty - you may have seen her around, visiting her aunt. Life is quite hard for her. She's back with her family now but she has very little money, and I know she'd like to come here and live with you, until the war ends."

Joss was silent for a few minutes. These arrangements were not uncommon; he knew of several men who kept Malayan mistresses, some of them on a long term basis. It was more usual for the man to ask his servant to find him someone, but not unknown for an offer to be made.

Taking his silence as an indication he was at least considering the offer, Khalish said:

"Would you like to meet her, *Tuan*, before you make up your mind?"

They agreed that the girl would come over the following evening.

Joss wrestled with his conscience that night and slept very little. Quite apart from being unfaithful to Gladys, the prospect of living in sin with a native girl - and quite possibly fathering a mixed race, illegitimate child - went totally against his strict Methodist upbringing. However, he could not help partly blaming Gladys for not standing up to Eliza, and was he really expected to live like a

49

monk until the war ended? It could go on for years and he might be unable to take home leave until it was over. He knew what his brother would think of the idea; William was much more straitlaced than he and inclined to be judgemental. He had thoroughly disapproved of Joss visiting brothels, when he had made the mistake of telling him about that in a letter. 'Deplorable sexual morals' was just one of the phrases he had used. If he went ahead with this arrangement, he could never tell Will nor, of course, Gladys. If there was a child of the union, he or she would have to be kept a secret from both his wife and his family. Nevertheless, despite his misgivings, he was sorely tempted. He had seen the girl around and she was not at all unattractive; he liked the idea of having her in his home and his bed.

When she arrived - a slightly built, brown-skinned girl with pleasing rounded features - he took her small, soft hand in his and asked her name, speaking in Malay.

"Alya."

"My first name is Joss. Do you want to come and live with me? No-one is forcing you into this, are they?"

She shook her head.

"You know that it can only be until the end of the war, at the latest? I am engaged to be married and, if I am transferred to one of the main towns before the war ends, I won't be able to take you with me. Of course, if we should have a child, I will support him or her and pay for English schooling."

She nodded her agreement. "I will try to make you happy, for as long as you want me."

Her subservience disturbed him, but he knew it was in keeping with the prevailing customs. He stilled the small voice inside him which told him he was exploiting her and resolved to treat her well and endeavour to make her happy for as long as they were together.

She brought her few things over and moved in. Watching her unpack, he realised how little she had. Peeling off a few dollar bills, he suggested she treat herself to some new outfits. Her eyes widened at the sight of so much money to be spent on clothes. He felt momentarily ashamed, as though he were buying her - which in a sense he was, although he told himself it was little different from keeping a wife.

He did not flaunt their relationship, as some men did with their Malayan mistresses. These were usually men who had no ambitions to rise above District Officer level. He went out and about without her, frequenting the club and playing tennis as usual after leaving his office, returning home in time for a quick sluice down with cold water before dinner. She had her limitations as a companion, compared to an English woman. She knew very little English and his Malay was not up to discussing anything complex. At first she spent the late evenings doing embroidery and other handicrafts, and he admired her work, which was exquisite. He read and wrote letters - feeling particularly guilty when writing to Gladys with Alya sitting opposite. One evening, she asked him if he would teach her English. He thought that was a very good idea, and something they could do together, so he obtained some books and they set to work, doing a lesson most evenings. She proved a quick learner and soon their conversation became a mixture of Malay and English. He also taught her to read and write English, although this progressed at a slower pace.

~ * ~

In early December 1914, Frank Healey married his sweetheart, Mary. Lavinia was a guest at the wedding and Gladys took the opportunity to ask her about the possibility of working in London for the duration of the war. Lavinia thought that there might be vacancies at the War Office; she believed they were taking on female staff to replace the men who had left to fight.

"I will make enquiries, and, if you do get a job in London, you can, of course, live with me."

Gladys thanked her - it would make a big difference financially if she did not have to rent a room. She was by no means sure that Henry would continue paying her allowance if she left home.

The War Office were taking on staff and in the New Year Gladys travelled to London for the interview, taking with her the various certificates she had obtained at school and college. These included bookkeeping, shorthand and typing, although her skills were rather rusty. She got the job, which involved working six days a week, with a full weekend off in every four. She would live with Lavinia in Bedford Place, but return home to visit her family on those weekends.

She relayed this news to Joss, who received it with rather mixed feelings. He was glad that she would have an occupation to see her through the war but would have preferred that it were not in London. He knew she would have a much more varied social life there than in Yorkshire and he was rather afraid that she might meet someone else. The irony of this was not lost on him, bearing in mind his present situation, but his heart was not involved with Alya. She was sweet and affectionate and he was becoming fond of her, but that was all.

Gladys found that she was working in a large office with many other women. She was a lowly clerk, and had to be deferential to the senior staff, who were all male. However, the work was not difficult and at times quite interesting and there was considerable camaraderie amongst the women during tea and lunch breaks. She found that having a fiance in the Malayan Colonial Government gave her a certain kudos.

~ * ~

In the spring of 1915, Alya started to experience early morning sickness. She realised straight away what this meant, but was unsure how Joss would take it. Initially concerned that she was ill, the truth eventually dawned on him, resulting in somewhat conflicting feelings. This was a far from ideal situation, but he had expected it would happen sooner or later and a part of him was not a little elated at the prospect of becoming a father. He became very solicitous of Alya, fussing over her when he was home, which she found rather amusing. She and her aunt worked out that the baby would probably be born in late October or early November.

When she was four or five months into her term, she reached for Joss' hand one evening and placed it on her belly.

"Can you feel?" Our baby is kicking!"

A slow smile spread over his face; this was his son or daughter in there, making their presence felt.

At the end of August, Joss received notification that he was to be transferred to Kuala Lumpur in mid September, to take over as magistrate on the civil side of the courts. He was dismayed; this was the worst possible timing - how could he leave Alya at that time, heavy with his unborn child? However, he could not take her with him to the capital. For one thing, as he was not married, he would not be allocated married quarters and would be sharing accommodation, and for another, the colonial service disapproved of concubinage, as it was called, and it would be a black mark against his record if it were discovered that he was keeping a Malayan mistress who was having his child, particularly as he was known to be engaged to a girl back in England. Joss knew he was already at a disadvantage when it came to being considered for future promotion to the most senior posts. He had not attended a public school and, as a scholarship student, had been a non-college undergraduate at Oxford. His academic achievements were considerable, but when it came down to it, the old boy network still prevailed at the higher levels of the service.

When he finally plucked up the courage to tell Alya they would have to part, her eyes filled with tears. He felt a complete heel and was full of remorse. He had used her and now he was discarding her. If he had done this to an Englishwoman he would have been labelled the worst kind of cad. His mother would turn in her grave if she knew, he thought. She had been so proud of him but now she would be thoroughly ashamed.

He tried to mitigate the situation by telling Alya he would not totally abandon her; he would come to see her as often as he could and always be there for her if she needed him. He would support the child until he or she was adult, paying for education at the English school in Klang. He asked her if she would be able to return to her family. She nodded.

"I'll take you back there, then, when the time comes, and try to explain to them. I'm so sorry," he added miserably.

Before he left he asked his assistant D.O., George, to keep an eye on her for him and let him know if there were any problems. He also wanted to know straight away once his child was born.

He made the round trip by train to Klang as often as he could and by a stroke of good luck was there when Alya's labour pains started and her waters broke. The village woman who acted as midwife was sent for and Joss sat in one room of the small, basic cottage where Alya's family lived, listening to her screams coming from the next room and feeling guiltier by the minute. Eventually, she was quiet and then he heard a baby's cry. A few minutes later, Alya's mother came out and placed a small bundle in his arms.

"You have a son; a fine boy."

Joss was quite unprepared for the sudden rush of feeling which overwhelmed him. This was his child, his flesh and blood, and he was responsible for his welfare. As he looked down at the tiny, trusting little face, he felt a tremendous surge of love and resolved to do everything in his power to protect him. He knew then that he could not be an absentee father and would always be a part of his son's life, however difficult this proved to be.

When they let him in to see Alya, he placed the baby carefully into her arms, pushed her damp hair back from her forehead and kissed her.

"You like him?" she asked anxiously.

"I love him! He's perfect! I want to be the best father I can to him. I'd like him to be baptised a Christian - will your family accept that?"

She thought they would not object.

"I also want to be on the birth certificate as his father and I'd like him to have English first names. Do you mind?"

She shook her head.

"What do you think of Theodore? Theo for short?"

"Theo," she repeated. "Yes, I like."

"And his middle name to be William, after my father and brother. I'll write it all down for you, to take with you when you register the birth."

As he looked again at the baby, he realised how light-skinned he was, and his features seemed much more English than Malayan. All the more reason to bring him up in as anglicised a way as possible, he thought, then he would have the best chance in life.

About six weeks after Theo's birth, Joss received a letter from his brother, announcing the birth of their latest child - another son, to be called Charles Stanley and known as Stanley. He noted the birth date, which was just a few days before Theo's. Two cousins the same age, he thought, who would sadly never meet.

Meanwhile, the war dragged on. In addition to the fighting in Europe, many ships had already been sunk, notably the Lusitania in May 1915, with the loss of 1198 passengers. There had been air raids in North and East London in the same month. Malaya had been relatively unaffected by the war, apart from a brief naval skirmish in October 1914 off the coast of Penang, between a German ship and a Russian cruiser, which had caused considerable local consternation at the time. Joss was a corporal in the Malay Volunteer Rifles and

55

they had been semi-mobilised since war was declared, but the only action he had seen so far was in February 1915 when an Indian regiment based in Singapore had mutinied. Thirty-five Europeans had been killed in that episode, but it had only lasted a few days.

Many of Joss' younger colleagues had left Malaya during the first six months of the war, in order to return to England and enlist. He and the others who remained had heavier workloads as a result and the authorities had entreated them to stay, as the country still needed to be governed. No new cadets had been taken on since the war started. Taking leave in England was more difficult now, owing to the shortage of staff to cover and the limited number of available ships, quite apart from the dangers of sailing in wartime. He had no idea when he would be able to take his next long leave, due in theory towards the end of 1916.

Conscription was brought in from January 1916 and then extended to married men in May. Joss feared for his brother. He was not too far off the upper age limit, so would not be one of the first to be called up, and perhaps may escape if the war did not go on for much longer. William wrote that Crossland and Ewart, Theresa's younger brothers, had been conscripted. That spring, they had both married their sweethearts, Ethel and Alice, and Will and Theresa had attended two weddings in quick succession. Gladys wrote that her cousin, Will Stocks, had been called up, but that Frank had so far escaped. One of Joss' friends, a fellow 1903 cadet, decided in 1916 to return to England to fight. Joss found himself scouring the casualty bulletins in the newspapers for the names of people he knew.

However, an unexpected death closer to home affected him first. His friend Ernie, another 1903 cadet, with whom he had shared a cabin on the voyage over and who had been posted with him to Seremban when they first arrived, was shot dead in February 1916. He was the Acting Resident of Brunei at the time. He had given chase, along with several others, when a Sikh sentry had attacked a colleague, and the man had turned and pulled out a gun. Everyone in the secretariat in Kuala Lumpur was shocked by his death and it was the talk of the club, but Joss was particularly affected as Ernie had been a close friend. Along with several others working in the capital, he travelled to Brunei to attend his memorial service and remembered sadly his previous visit there, when he and Ernie had had a good time together.

~ * ~

Meanwhile, back in England, Gladys had a growing sense of unease about her relationship with Joss. Time and distance were taking their toll and she felt that their spiritual bond was fraying. She fancied that Joss' protestations of love were becoming more mechanical than heartfelt; he seemed to be holding something back of himself, no longer sharing unreservedly his innermost thoughts and feelings. The change in tone in his letters was very subtle and she told herself she may be imagining it, or perhaps he was responding to a perceived change of tone in her letters; was she starting to write more as a friend than a lover? She tried to correct this the next time she wrote. Then she received his letter telling her about his friend's death and he seemed to be reaching out to her once more. He described his sadness and reminisced about their early friendship, mentioning how supportive Ernie had been to him following his mother's death. He told Gladys how much he needed her and wished that she were with him.

" ..... *Never doubt that I love you as much as ever, my darling, despite the years and miles between us. I am sometimes afraid that you'll meet someone else in London and break off our engagement, and I couldn't bear to lose you. Please wait for us to be together again; this war cannot go on forever!....*"

~ * ~

In addition to long home leaves, all government officials were entitled to a couple of weeks a year local leave. In the past, Joss had used his to visit Singapore or Siam or visit friends based in the further flung parts of the colony, and had only once before taken a break in one of the hill stations. These were holiday resorts in the mountains, where the air was cooler and fresher, and provided a welcome respite from the heat and humidity of the lowlands.

In early October 1916, he decided to take his overdue local leave and booked two weeks in Bukit Kutu, being the nearest hill station to Kuala Lumpur. After having ascertained that no senior government officials had reserved any of the accommodation for that period, he took Alya and Theo with him. Ostensibly, Alya was part of his household staff and she did in fact do most of the cooking, assisted by Joss' houseboy. She shared Joss' bed, although full relations were not resumed as they did not want to risk conceiving another child. He socialised with the other Europeans holidaying there, frequenting the club and playing sports and card games, but inside their bungalow, he and Alya and Theo behaved as a family. Theo was now eleven months old and a happy gurgling baby; his besotted father found him a joy to be with. He never tired of talking to him and playing baby games. With his light-honey coloured skin, mid brown hair and blue eyes, he could easily pass for a British child.

Watching them together, Alya said:

"He looks very like you. He has your eyes."

He could now walk a little, holding on to Joss' or Alya's hands, and repeat some words spoken to him. Joss had brought some picture books with him and he pointed to the objects and animals portrayed and told Theo the English words for them. He hoped his son would grow up speaking English almost as well as Malayan.

The New Year of 1917 dawned and there was still no end to the war in sight. America entered the conflict in April, which gave cause for optimism, but there was increasing submarine warfare and further air raids in southern England. However, more countries were severing relations with Germany and some also declared war, although Russia had withdrawn.

Joss was becoming increasingly concerned that he and Gladys were growing apart. He knew it was probably inevitable, given the fact that they had now been separated for five years and had only spent four months together. Living with Alya and having Theo had not helped, he knew, and Gladys' letters indicated she was having quite a good time in London, socialising both with her colleagues at the war office and Lavinia's circle of friends. Whilst he was pleased for her that she was broadening her horizons - he knew how she had chafed against the restrictions of her life in Yorkshire - he was afraid that her new life may have changed her. His own social life was much as it had been before he had met her, Alya and Theo apart, but hers was now very different.

He needed to take his home leave and get back to England as soon as he could. He made his application and eventually received the response that he could take six months leave, commencing with the next available sailing after October. That proved to be in early January 1918, with a return passage in July, sailing via Japan. This was a single return passage only; he would be sharing a cabin with another male passenger. Gladys would still have to wait to join him until the war ended, but at least they could be married, assuming that they both still wanted that when they finally met again.

Joss did not really mind that he had only been granted six months leave. Only the first six months was on full pay; the second reduced to half pay. As he now had Theo to support, he did not want to reduce his income. In addition, he did not want to be away from his son for any longer; as it was, he would be missing many milestones in his early development.

In the weeks leading up to his departure, he tried to prepare Theo for his absence. He was now two years old and used to seeing Joss weekly.

"Daddy has to sail over the sea to England on a big ship and I'll be away for a while, but I'll be thinking of you all the time and I'll send you lots of picture postcards."

To Alya, he said: "Please talk to him in English some of the time - your English is quite good now - and tell him constantly that I love him and don't want to be away from him. And when the postcards arrive, read them to him and tell him they are from me. Please keep my existence alive in his memory."

"Are you bringing your wife back with you?" she asked.

"No. She'll have to stay there until the war ends."

"And when she does come, will you still be able to see Theo every week?"

"I don't know; it may have to be less. I'll make it as often as I can. It will also depend on where I am based. One day, perhaps I'll be able to tell Gladys about Theo, if we manage to have our own child. If we don't, I think I'll never be able to tell her."

The last time he visited them, he took a camera with him and took several pictures of Theo. He would take one or two with him, keeping them well hidden in his luggage. He handed Alya enough money to tide her over and then hugged Theo goodbye. He could hardly bear to leave, knowing that the child might not recognise him on his return and he may have to rebuild their relationship from scratch. His sadness communicated itself to Theo, who started to cry.

"Watch me going down the road and wave bye-bye," Joss said, to distract him, and gave him one final kiss before tearing himself away.

On the train on the way back to Kuala Lumpur, he reflected on his earlier conversation with Alya. It was true that, as Gladys would be thirty-nine in February, they may not find it too easy to conceive a child. As long as he still felt the same about her, he could accept that, but if he didn't? Or she about him? He could hardly break off their engagement if she still wanted it, not when she had waited so long for him. He hoped all would be as before, then the issue would not arise. That their friendship would have survived he had no doubt - their letters had kept that alive - but could the embers of their earlier passion be reignited? Would the dreams and fantasies, which had sustained them over the last six years, match up with the reality of seeing each other again?

~ * ~

Gladys was overjoyed to receive his letter advising of his leave, along with his date & port of arrival, which was Saturday 16th February 1918 at Liverpool.   However, she noted with disappointment that it was only for six months this time and that she would not be able to return with him. She was also rather puzzled that he had made no mention of arrangements for their wedding, but presumably he intended them to discuss that face to face once he arrived. It was probably a good idea to have a little time to court each other again before they married. She also had her doubts that their relationship could immediately take up where it had left off, but as long as the friendship and affection remained, she was confident that love would soon grow again between them, although perhaps a quieter, calmer love than before. She still missed him and longed to be reunited with him, but it had almost become a habit. The reality was that she had got used to living her life without him.

She arranged to take her full weekend off a week earlier than usual, so she could come up to Yorkshire on the Friday evening and go to Liverpool to meet him that Saturday morning. She also booked a day of her annual leave for the Monday so they would have more time together initially. The rest of her leave she would save for her wedding and honeymoon.

~ * ~

Chapter 6

As the morning of the 16th February dawned, both Joss and Gladys woke filled with nervous anticipation. Joss was up on deck early and watched as the Lancashire coastline came into view. By then, Gladys had already embarked on her train journey from Brighouse to Liverpool.

As he disembarked, Joss scanned the waiting crowds for Gladys, but could not see her. He heard someone say that the train had been delayed. He went to locate his trunk and have it sent on to Heckmondwike and then returned to the main dock area. Still there was no sign of her. He asked about the train, and was told it had now arrived. Was she not coming after all? Disappointment swept through him.

Then he saw her, running towards him, waving madly. He picked up his case and ran too, weaving through the crowds. As they met, they fell into each others' arms, and suddenly he was back in 1911 and all the love he had felt for her flooded back. Her touch was the same, her scent was the same; she was laughing and crying simultaneously, and he just held on to her. When they finally broke apart, he cupped her face in his hands and said huskily:

"I was so afraid......"

"That it wouldn't be the same," she finished for him. "I was too. But it is, isn't it? We're still us."

On the train, they sat side by side, holding hands tightly, drinking in the details of each other and registering the little changes which six years had wrought. He was relieved that she had not cut her hair, as he had heard some women had done since the war started, and he liked the shorter above-ankle length skirt she was wearing. He noticed a few fine lines at the corner of her eyes, but they in no way detracted from her beauty. She, in turn, noticed that he now had quite a few fine lines around his eyes and mouth - the tropical climate was less kind on skin - and he looked as though he may have put on a few pounds, but she found the changes appealing. The small amount of extra weight somehow made him seem more solid and safe. She squeezed him around the middle.

"I see there's now a little more of you!"

He grinned. "I hope you don't mind? It's from doing a desk job in Kuala Lumpur the last couple of years. Out in the districts, I get more exercise during the working day."

"No, I like it - there's more to cuddle!"

"And I like it that you're now showing more of your lovely legs and I'm really glad you didn't cut your beautiful hair!"

Hesitantly, she said: "I know you'll want to spend time with your family as well as with me, but seeing as I'm in London most of the time, I hope you'll be able to spend part of each week with me there? Aunt Lavinia says there'll be a room ready for you whenever you want to come. Perhaps you could travel down on Saturdays so we can spend Saturday evening and Sunday together? "

"That sounds fine," he assured her. "Will you continue to work there after we're married?"

She felt a flash of relief that he had brought up their marriage. "I was planning to, yes. Until I can travel to Malaya, which I suppose won't be until this war ends. I feel that I'm doing something useful for the war effort. You don't mind, do you?" she added anxiously.

"Of course not."

She told him he was invited over to her parents' house for Sunday and then added: "Shall we start making plans for our wedding? I'd like it to be in Brighouse Methodist chapel, if that's alright with you? I was baptised a Methodist and my family all attend that chapel."

"I was also brought up as a Methodist, so that's fine with me."

"Really? I thought you were Church of England. You all went to Heckmondwike parish church."

"Will switched after he married Theresa, and I believe our father was Anglican, but, as children, we were both taken to the Methodist chapel by our mother. When I was living at Will's, I just went to the same church they did - it's all the same God, after all! I must confess that in Malaya I go to neither church nor chapel very often."

"Neither do I, in London."

After a pause, she said: "I think you can only have banns called in the Church of England and we'll have to get a licence."

"You may well be right. And there might be a problem with neither of us being resident in Brighouse. We can go and check out the position on Monday. How long do you think we need to organise everything?"

"My mother says we'll need at least three months! And I do have to get a dress made, and dresses for the bridesmaids - oh, I wondered if Mabel would like to be one of them?"

"I expect she would. You can ask her. You are staying the rest of the day with me in Heckmondwike, aren't you?"

"If Will and Theresa won't mind."

"I'm sure they won't. So, we are looking at a May wedding?"

"Yes, I think so. I can also take the rest of my annual leave then, so we can have a honeymoon. I can't take it earlier - there're a lot of silly rules which apply to the junior staff. After we're married we can both live mainly at Lavinia's - she's already offered. She'll allow us to share a room then!"

The train arrived at Huddersfield station, where they had to change. They had a carriage to themselves on the final short leg of the journey and took the opportunity to indulge in some long lingering kisses and cuddle up close together.

"I can hardly believe that you're really here and we're finally together again!" she said. "It's like a dream come true!"

As they turned the corner into Church Lane, where William and his family now lived, they saw that one of the houses had a brightly coloured banner across the top of the door. As they came closer, they saw that it was the house they were heading for and the banner read ' Welcome Home Uncle Joss.' Touched by the gesture, he had to swallow hard.

As they arrived outside the door, it opened and Mabel ran out and into his arms. She was now ten years old, but he could still see in her the four year old he had known. She was followed by Donald, now twelve, who shook hands with Joss enthusiastically. William appeared in the doorway, smiling.

"Let him get inside, will you!"

He greeted Gladys, then put an arm affectionately across his brother's shoulders and briefly laid his cheek against his.

"It's really good to see you again. I'm glad you made it safely - we were worried about submarines!" He ushered them all inside.

After greeting his sister-in-law, Joss was introduced to Ewart, now five and a half, and Stanley, who reminded him forcibly of his own Theo. He reintroduced himself to Leslie, who predictably did not remember him. He was now a bespectacled eight and a half year old.

"I hear that you're learning the cello and becoming very good," Joss told him. "I'd love to hear you play!"

"You'll soon get fed up of hearing it!" Donald declared. "He has to practice most evenings."

The table in the back room was laid ready for the midday meal. Will had taken the afternoon off from the shop.

"You will join us, Gladys, won't you?" Theresa asked. "And stay for tea too."

Gladys thanked her and accepted.

"You're in the front room again," Will said. "Don and I have already put up the bed and Theresa has cleared some drawers for you. We still don't use that room very much, although Leslie does his cello practice in there."

Joss went to unpack his case, then returned. The house was a little larger than the one in Cambridge Street, with an extra bedroom, and he knew from Will's letters that they had bought the property, with the aid of a loan from the bank. Will & Theresa were now home owners. He reflected that, in some respects, his brother had climbed further up the worldly ladder than he had, despite his Oxford education. This impression was further compounded by Theresa saying that he would not yet know Will's latest news; he was shortly to be made a director of the company he worked for. Joss and Gladys congratulated him.

"Well, the extra money will help to pay the mortgage on this place!"

Over the meal, Theresa asked about their wedding plans.

"We've only just started to talk about it, on the train," Gladys said, "but it looks like it will be around May and at the Bethel Road chapel in Brighouse."

She turned to Mabel. "Would you like to be one of my bridesmaids?"

"Oh, yes! I'd love to."

"I'd like you to be my best man," Joss told his brother, "but I'd also like you to play the organ, and you probably can't do both."

"I suppose you could have someone else do the best man's duties in the chapel," Theresa suggested, "and Will could still do the rest - stag night, speech and so on."

"That's an idea, but I can't think who. I've only kept in touch with a few chaps here and they are all away, fighting."

"Frank would probably do it, if you like," Gladys suggested. "We could ask him tomorrow - he'll be joining us for lunch."

"So you're at the Healeys' tomorrow?" Will asked.

"Yes, but I'll come to church with you all first."

The children told Joss they were all on half-term holiday the following week.

"That's good. It'll give me a chance to spend some time with you all, as from Tuesday, when Gladys has gone back. On Saturday, I'll be going down to London, to stay with Gladys at her aunt's, returning on Monday morning. I'll be doing that most weeks."

"So we'll see rather less of you this time, then," Will observed.

"Can't be helped, I'm afraid."

After tea, Leslie went to do his music practice and soon the opening strains of one of the Bach cello suites drifted out of the front room.

"He's very good!" Joss exclaimed.

"Yes, not bad for an eight year old," Will said, with no small degree of pride.

Donald snorted. "He's been practising that one for months!"

It was now dark outside and Joss told Gladys he would accompany her back on the train.

"No need. If I'm not home by seven, Father will come to collect me. He's now the proud owner of a motor car!"

"Gosh," Ewart said. "Can we have a ride in it?"

"You'll have to ask him. I daresay he might drive you all round the block. If you admire the car, he'll be more likely to oblige - it's a new toy and his pride and joy!"

"Why can't we get a car, Dad?" Ewart asked.

"Because we can't afford one! Perhaps in about ten years time, if they've become cheaper and if you lot haven't bankrupted me by then!"

Henry tooted his horn, and they all trooped out to admire the car, which was parked under the streetlight. It was indeed a splendid, gleaming piece of machinery. Henry was looking older, Joss thought. His hair, which had been streaked with grey, was now almost completely white. They shook hands.

"It's good to see you again!" Henry said. "Is all well between the two of you? Wedding still going ahead?"

"Indeed it is," Joss assured him.

"I need to apologise to you, and so does my wife, as she'll tell you herself tomorrow. We were the primary cause of you two being kept apart for so long, before the war. We've made our peace with Gladys, and I hope you can also forgive us."

Joss assured him it was all in the past and he bore them no grudge. Then he joined the boys in admiring the car.

"Do you have a car in Malaya?" Henry asked.

"No, but I have the use of one when I'm working out in the Districts. Nothing like as nice as this, though!"

Impatiently, Ewart interrupted, asking if they could have a drive in it.

"Yes, of course you can, young man. I'll take you all round the block. Hop in!"

All five of them managed to squash in, Donald in front with Henry and Stanley sitting on Mabel's lap.

"Keep a firm hold of him, Mabel," Theresa said anxiously. "And you two, stay sitting down!" This to Ewart and Leslie.

"Don't worry," Henry said. "I won't be going fast enough for them to come to any harm."

After they had returned, Gladys got into the car and Joss leaned over the door to kiss her.

"I'll see you tomorrow - and I haven't forgotten it's your birthday!"

In the evening, the children went to bed in stages, in order of age. After Donald had gone up, Theresa announced that she was quite tired and bid them goodnight.

"You've got five wonderful children, Will," Joss said. "I envy you your family."

"Well, hopefully you'll have one or two of your own before long."

"Maybe. Gladys will be thirty-nine tomorrow, so we're cutting it fine."

He had a sudden, almost irresistible urge to say: ' Actually, I do have a son; he's called Theo and he's the same age as Stanley.' He stopped himself just in time. It would be a monumental mistake. Apart from the recriminations which would be heaped upon his head, there was always the danger that either Will or Theresa would think it their duty to tell Gladys.

Changing the subject, he said. "I'm glad that you've not been called up. I was quite worried about that."

"Well, I still might be. I'm not out of the woods yet. Meanwhile, I'm now in the Volunteer Training Force, for home defence duties - a bit like your Malay Volunteer Rifles."

"Hopefully, they'll leave you doing that. Any news of Crossland and Ewart?"

"They're both on the front line but as far as we know they're still alive. Theresa worries about them a lot, as do their wives, of course."

"What about George?"

"He's escaped so far, like me." A thought struck him. "Now you're back in England, are you liable to be conscripted?"

"No, because I'm not normally resident in England."

"That's a relief!"

"Part of me feels perhaps I ought to have volunteered," Joss said. "Fight for King and country and all that!"

"Leave it to the younger ones. Between you and me, I'm by no means sure that we should be in this war at all."

After church the next morning, Joss made his way to Brighouse. As Henry had done, Eliza anxiously asked him to forgive her for delaying Gladys' departure before the war. He reassured her that it was all in the past now. He saw that she too was looking her age, with a substantial amount of grey in her dark hair and definite lines around her eyes and mouth. He was introduced to Frank's wife, Mary, an attractive, fair haired young woman.

Over the meal, Eliza brought up the wedding and they told her what they had agreed so far. She asked Gladys about her dress, and whether she wanted their usual dressmaker to do it.

"No, I'll go to Lavinia's dressmaker in London, but I'd be really grateful if you could take care of the bridesmaids' outfits, Mother. I'll have my friend Celia as Matron of Honour and her daughter and

Mabel as bridesmaids; they're about the same age. Perhaps you could liaise with Celia and Theresa? I know material is scarce, but hopefully we can all find something."

"Once you've booked the chapel, we'll need to sort out a venue for the reception," Henry said. "By the way, the cost of the wedding is all on me, Joss. All you need to buy is the ring!"

Joss thanked him.

"You'll need to let us know who you're inviting from your side," Eliza said. "Besides Will and Theresa and their children. Are there to be any other guests? Wider family, old school friends?"

Joss shook his head. "Those few friends I've kept in contact with are all away fighting and I've lost touch with the wider family - anyway, most of the older generation are dead."

Gladys interjected. "We don't need to invite all the relatives on our side either. I've hardly seen any of them for years, apart from Aunt Lavinia and cousin Ethel. Let's just have them, and if cousin Will happens to be on leave, of course he can come too. Otherwise, just us and a few of my friends."

"Well, this wedding is getting cheaper by the minute!" Henry joked. "I suppose, as it's wartime, a lavish do would be inappropriate anyway."

Frank agreed to take over the best man's duties in the chapel while Will was playing the organ. "As long as I don't have to do the speech!"

"I'd almost rather you did that too," Joss said, grinning. "You wouldn't be able to recount embarrassing episodes from my youth!"

Whilst they were talking, Joss had noticed a subtle change in Gladys' relationship with her parents; a slight power shift. She was no longer the junior member of the clan; she was an equal with them. Her years in London had given her a self assurance she had not had before. He thought wryly that there would now be no way that Eliza or Henry could stop her going to Malaya - what a pity this had not been the case earlier.

The following morning, Joss and Gladys went to see the Methodist minister. To their dismay, all the chapel's available dates for weddings in May were already booked, and the same applied to April and well into June. The first free date was on Monday 24th June. Otherwise, it would have to be prior to Easter, which was at the end of March that year.

"The June date only gives us a month of marriage before I return," Joss said, "but I suppose March is too soon to organise everything."

"Yes, and I wouldn't be able to take my two weeks leave then."

After a little further deliberation, they decided on 24th June. The minister confirmed they would need a licence, which they would both have to apply for in their respective registration districts, one of which would have to be Brighouse.

"So one of you will need to live here for seven days prior to giving notice to the registrar."

"That will have to be you, darling," Gladys said. "You can stay with my parents; they have plenty of room."

The minister continued: "You'll also need to live there for fifteen days before the wedding. And don't apply for the licence too soon, as it's only valid for three months."

They returned to the Healeys'. Henry was also there, as he was now semi-retired from the factory, leaving most of the day to day running to Frank. They expressed themselves delighted to have Joss stay for a week in early April and then again for two weeks before the wedding.

"You can have Frank's old room."

Gladys returned to London that evening and Joss saw her off at Brighouse station. Kissing goodbye was a prolonged affair, neither of them wanting to part again so soon, even for a few days.

The next afternoon, Joss took Ewart and Leslie to the cinema in Halifax to see a comedy western. Donald had arranged something with his friends and Mabel had said she did not much like westerns.

71

They all enjoyed the film and Joss treated the boys to ice-creams afterwards, in the nearby ice-cream parlour.

"Do you have cinemas in Malaya?" Leslie asked.

Joss told him that there was now one in Kuala Lumpur, but that he had only been to it once.

The following day, being fine weather, they all went for a walk, including Donald and Mabel. By the end of the week, he felt he was getting to know them.

First thing on Saturday, Joss set off for London. Gladys finished work earlier on Saturdays and he had told her he would meet her outside her office. Having dropped his overnight bag off at Bedford Place, greeted Lavinia and thanked her for allowing him to stay, he arrived at the War Office in Whitehall just before four o'clock. The staff started to emerge and shortly afterwards she appeared, flanked by two other women. She ran over to him and they kissed.

"So this is your beau from Malaya!" one of the women observed.

Gladys introduced them.

"We've heard a lot about you!" the one called Mathilda said.

"All good, I hope!"

They decided to walk back to Bloomsbury, rather than take the underground, the weather being dry. Now Joss was in London, he was reminded of how he had worried for her when he had heard of air raids on the capital.

"There could still be more of them, although they seem to have eased off for the present."

"Well, in the war office, they are saying it could all be over by the end of the year."

"Let's hope they're right."

As they went through Trafalgar Square and up Shaftesbury Avenue, he saw several shops selling picture postcards, and spotted one showing a London bus, which Theo would like. He made a mental note to buy a few cards on his way home on Monday and write one of them on the train. He had already sent Theo one with a picture of the ship, posting it when they had docked en route. He also intended, at some point, to get him some presents, which he would have to wrap well and secrete at the bottom of his trunk. He hated having to be secretive and hide Theo's existence from Gladys, but apart from the fear that she would leave him if she found out, he did not want to cause her pain. He knew she would be terribly hurt, not only because of his infidelity but because he had had a child by someone else, when it may possibly be too late for her to conceive. He could not help wondering whether she had any doubts that he had remained faithful to her over the last six years. She was no fool and may well guess that he had strayed once or twice, but probably assumed that it was only an occasional casual liaison, perhaps with a discontented married woman. It was highly unlikely that she would view with equanimity the existence of a native mistress.

They arrived back at Bedford Pace in time to take tea with Lavinia. Gladys told her they would be out for dinner as she had tickets for the theatre.

"I'll have cook leave you out a light supper," Lavinia said. "I'm out for dinner myself. By the way, you'll have noticed that Joss' room is across the landing from yours, Gladys. Mine is in between and I am a very light sleeper. I daresay you're both itching to anticipate your marriage vows, but I'd prefer that you don't do it in my house!"

They both reddened and muttered assent.

The play was a comedy and they were both still chortling as they came out of the theatre. Back home, they tucked into cook's idea of a light supper.

"You'd never think that they'd just introduced rationing in London, would you!" Gladys said.

Lavinia still being out, they sat on the sofa in the drawing room and kissed and caressed each other, until the sound of the front door opening caused them to spring apart and hastily straighten their clothes. Lavinia looked at them in some amusement; Gladys was still trying to replace the pins in her hair.

"What I said earlier didn't mean you can't cuddle up on the sofa!" she said, laughing.

They spent Sunday looking around some of the sights of London, hand in hand, wrapped up well against the cold wind.

The next few weeks sped by in much the same vein. The four older children were at school, but Joss took Stanley to the park on several occasions. During his second week, he was introduced to Theresa's cleaning lady, Edna. Upon Theresa telling her he was getting married in June, she shook her head sagely and said:

"Aye, there'll be many a bright eye dimmed before then!"

At teatime, when he recounted this strange comment to the rest of the family, they all laughed.

"She says that all the time!" Leslie told him.

"Yes, if anyone mentions anything in the future, she comes out with that phrase," Donald said, and Will added "She's a real harbinger of doom!"

Ewart told Joss they were soon to get a dog.

"I said *maybe* we could get one, perhaps for Christmas," Will corrected.

"Not if I'm going to be the only one looking after him," Theresa declared. "You will all have to take him for walks."

"I will," Ewart promised. "I'll get up early and take him before school."

"As long as I don't have to get up early!" Leslie said, looking horror-struck at the thought.

"Fat chance!" Donald said, laughing. "You have to be kicked out of bed to even get to school on time!"

Joss sometimes travelled down to London on Friday or stayed over until Tuesday, to give him more time with Gladys. The weekend before Easter was Gladys' next Saturday off, so she was in Yorkshire two weekends running. They spend Easter Sunday at

Heckmondwike and that evening Joss packed his case and returned with her to Brighouse, to start his week's residence there. Before she returned to London, she asked him if he was still coming down at the weekend.

"Will it violate your seven days residence if you're not here every night?"

Joss had no idea, but Henry thought it would not matter; as long as Joss came and went from their address, he would still be classed as living there, and anyway, who, apart from them, would know?

"However, perhaps you had better return on the Sunday evening so you're only away one night."

Listening to Gladys talking to Eliza about her wedding dress, Joss suddenly wondered what she had planned to wear in Malaya, had that wedding gone ahead.

"I had a thin white cotton dress and a wide-brimmed hat," she told him. "I thought that would be more suitable for such a hot climate. It wouldn't have done for a March wedding here, if that's what you're thinking!"

Joss' birthday on 3rd May fell on a Friday that year. Mabel had asked him not to go to London until Saturday so that he would be with them for tea. She had baked him a cake and had decorated it - mostly by herself, Theresa said - with 'Happy Birthday Uncle Joss' and added four candles, one slightly shorter than the others.

"You've made him four years old!" Leslie said, and Ewart giggled.

"Don't be daft! Each candle is ten years and the shorter one is eight years. Dad said he's thirty-eight."

"It's a beautiful cake," Joss assured her. "Thank you."

It tasted good too and Theresa remarked that she could do more baking in future and give her a well-earned rest!

The Whitsun bank holiday on 20th May coincided with one of Gladys' long weekends. The Saturday had also been designated a bank holiday that year which gave her an extra day to take later on.

The weather had turned dry and fairly warm, so she and Joss decided to take a day trip up to the moors. Finding a secluded spot, off the beaten track, they spread out a picnic blanket to lie on, as they had done in 1911, but this time they were less constrained by the prospect of possible repercussions and let their instincts take over until they finally came together completely.

As they basked in the drowsy, love-drenched aftermath, Gladys suddenly said:

"You weren't a virgin, were you." It was a statement, rather than a question.

"No," he admitted, hoping she would not ask for details.

"Tell me about the first time."

He breathed easier; this was fairly safe ground. "It was in my second year at Oxford, with a widowed friend of my landlady who was staying for the weekend. She and I sat up playing cards and drinking, after the others had gone to bed, and one thing led to another. She was about fifteen years older than me and taught me quite a lot!"

"Were you in love with her?"

"No, but I liked her. I told you, I've never been in love with anyone but you; you are my soul mate." He stroked her face and planted feathery light kisses on her lips and nose.

She snuggled up closer against him and did not pursue the subject. She did not really want to know if there had been anyone during the last six years, nor did she want to give him cause to have to lie to her. It was enough that he had never loved anyone else. Then she said:

"I wonder if we've already made a baby?"

"I suppose it's possible. If so, will we have to pretend its arrival is one month early?!"

"I doubt that would fool anyone! I think a baby born a month early would be quite small and might not even live."

"Actually, my brother was born only two months after our parents married."

"Really?"

"Yes, he only found out after our mother died and he was clearing out the house. He found their marriage certificate and some photographs of their wedding which showed Mum as a rather plump bride! He was not best pleased. You'd better not let on that I told you. He asked me to keep it quiet, pillar of the church that he is now!"

When Gladys returned to London after the long weekend, she found that the Germans had carried out further air raids during the Sunday night. She saw quite a few newly damaged buildings as she made her way by bus from Kings Cross to Bedford Place. Luckily the properties there were all unscathed. When Joss heard the news, he worried anew about her being in London, as did Eliza, and for once they were in accord.

Two weeks before their wedding date, Joss borrowed Henry's car and moved all his things over to the Healeys' home. He would stay the night immediately before the wedding back in Heckmondwike, but would otherwise be dividing his time between Brighouse and London until his return to Malaya. He assured Will that he would come over to them regularly during the next two weeks and he and Gladys would be frequent visitors thereafter whenever they were in Yorkshire.

"I'll probably also pop up from London for a night or two midweek. You haven't got rid of me yet!"

Gladys' next Saturday off was due on 15th June, but she carried it forward to the following weekend to give her more time in Yorkshire immediately before the wedding. They had had no further opportunity to make love, but when Joss arrived in London that Saturday for a one night visit, Gladys greeted him excitedly with the news that Lavinia was away for the weekend.

"We'd better be careful that the servants don't suspect anything, in case they report to her, but they sleep on the floor above and no-one has the bedroom immediately above mine - I checked - so you could tiptoe across to my room after they've all gone to bed. You'd have to leave early in the morning before the maid brings the tea, but we could spend most of the night together!"

After dinner, they cuddled up on the sofa, desire building, until they judged it was late enough. Joss went to his room initially, then crept softly across the landing and tapped on her door. She had changed into a long flimsy nightdress and her hair was loose and falling over her shoulders. He clasped her in his arms, then gently lifted the nightgown over her head and stepped back to admire her naked body.

"You are so beautiful!"

She pulled open his dressing gown and he slipped it off. They fell onto the bed, bodies entwined.

Sometime after dawn had broken, Gladys woke and turned towards him. He was still fast asleep. She stroked his face and kissed him, then slid her hand lower down. He woke in a state of arousal and reached for her.

Afterwards, she whispered. "You need to go back to your room. It's half-past six."

He groaned. "Must I? I want to stay in bed with you forever, touching you and holding you and making love over and over!"

"I want that too, but we can't! We'll have to wait until our honeymoon - we can spend the whole of it in bed!"

"I can't wait! I love you to distraction!"

~ * ~

Chapter 7

On the Friday evening before the wedding, Will had arranged a modest stag night. As so few younger men were available, the party consisted of only Joss and Will, Frank Healey, Will Stocks, who was on leave, and George Mallinson. (Joss had added some of Theresa's family to the guest list). Henry had been invited to join them but had declined, saying he was too old for such things. They adjourned to a local inn.

"Don't let me drink too much," Joss warned his brother.

"You've got time to recover before the wedding!"

"Yes, but Gladys will be back from London tonight and I don't want to greet her in a befuddled state."

He was also concerned that, if he became too inebriated, he might let something slip about Theo. That would be disastrous, especially in Gladys' brother's presence.

The evening before the wedding, Joss went over to Heckmondwike to stay the night there. Henry had organised cars to collect them all in the morning, one for Joss and William and one for Theresa and the boys. Mabel was staying the night in Brighouse, being one of the bridesmaids. The children were all delighted to have the day off school.

After the boys and Theresa had all gone up to bed, Will said: "Well, this is your last night of freedom!"

"That's such a terrible cliche!"

"You've no last-minute doubts, then?"

"None at all. I've waited a long time for this."

"I'm glad that it's finally worked out for you. I want you to be happy and I hope you will be. Marriage isn't always a bed of roses but I for one would not be single again."

Joss looked across at his brother and wished again that he could tell him about Theo. Keeping his secret from both him and Gladys was becoming an ever greater burden. He could now see the attraction of the Catholic religion: to be able to confess all and have your sins forgiven, with no repercussions! He wanted Will to know that he had a nephew and he wanted Theo to meet his family in England one day, but how was that ever going to be possible? He did not seriously think that Will would disown him - their brotherly bond was too strong for that - but Theresa would certainly cool towards him and they may not want their children to have anything to do with a half-caste illegitimate cousin. And he might not be able to dissuade them from telling Gladys.

Watching the turmoil cross his face, Will asked: "What is it, Joss?"

"Nothing." He smiled. "I was just thinking ahead to our honeymoon."

"Rubbish! That wasn't pleasant anticipation I saw on your face! You forget how well I know you. You were debating whether to tell me something. I had the same feeling the first night you were here."

"You're wrong, there's nothing."

"I don't believe you, but it's up to you whether to say anything, whatever it is. Just know that I'm always here for you."

Joss felt a sudden surge of affection for him. "You're the best brother a chap could have, do you know that?"

"Well, I would give you that accolade too, so we're well-suited, aren't we?!"

They arrived at the Bethel chapel in Elland Road in good time, both dressed in their best dark, three-piece suits. William needed to be a little early, to prepare for his organist role. Frank arrived next.

"Have you got the ring?" he asked Joss.

"Of course." He took the little box out of his pocket.

William began to warm up on the organ, the Minister arrived and then the guests started to enter. Joss felt the first flutter of nerves;

what if she had had second thoughts and did not turn up? As if guessing his thoughts, Frank said:

"Don't worry, she'll be here."

He heard Will play the opening bars of Handel's 'Arrival of the Queen of Sheba' which Gladys had chosen for her walk down the aisle, scorning the usual 'Here comes the bride' tune. He turned and saw her enter the chapel on Henry's arm, Celia and the two girls following, all dressed in blue. He watched her progress down the aisle towards him, in her demure white dress, a long veil covering her face, and suddenly thought:

"She's too good for me! I'm not worthy of her!"

He was not aware he had muttered the words out loud until Frank hissed in his ear:

"Don't talk daft! She's no angel, I can assure you!"

Then she was there, by his side, and he felt so much love for her he thought he might burst.

Gladys had had her own last minute fear that he might have had a change of heart. Had it been a mistake to give herself to him before the wedding? She was much relieved to see him standing there, waiting for her. She slipped her hand into his and he gave it a squeeze.

After an initial hymn, the Minister started on his preamble. When he asked those assembled if they knew of any impediment to their marriage, Joss could not help thinking of Alya. She was no legal impediment, but could be said to be a moral one. When it was his turn to be asked whether he took Gladys to be his lawful wedded wife... ..'forsaking all others'.....he said fervently: "I do" and resolved never to be unfaithful to her again. They both intoned their vows, promising to love and cherish each other.......'for better, for worse, for richer, for poorer, in sickness and in health.......until death us do part'. Joss took the ring from Frank and slipped it onto Gladys' finger, repeating the words spoken by the Minister: "With this ring I thee wed, with my body I thee honour, and with all my worldly goods I thee endow."

Finally they were pronounced husband and wife and adjourned to the vestry to sign the register, along with Frank and Henry who were the witnesses. As they came out of the chapel, Gladys with her veil now thrown back, Joss turned to her in the porch and told her how incredibly beautiful she looked.

"You're looking pretty handsome yourself," she said, smiling.

After photographs had been taken outside the chapel and liberal amounts of confetti had been thrown at them, they made their way to the Royal Hotel. This was one of Brighouse's most prestigious hotels, which in 1907 had entertained royalty in the form of Princess Louise. The best wedding feast that the hotel could provide in wartime had been laid on.

"Welcome to our family!" Theresa said to Gladys, and then added: "That's a lovely dress!"

It was indeed and several of the other women were also admiring it. Ankle-length and fairly full skirted, it was made of silk with lace panels and had long sleeves and a V neckline. Her train and veil were of the same lace, and her headdress was in the fashionable mob cap style.

"You were lucky to be able to get this material," Celia said.

"I have Aunt Lavinia's dressmaker to thank for that. I don't know how she managed it."

The bridesmaids' dresses were also lovely, and Joss told Mabel how pretty she looked.

After the meal, the speeches began. William began, as predicted, by detailing some of Joss' more amusing boyhood scrapes, then went on to praise his achievements. To his brother's embarrassment, he recounted how their mother had kept a scrap book of cuttings from the Huddersfield Chronicle, reporting on Almondbury Grammar School's annual prize-giving day, when Joss had invariably scooped the lion's share of the prizes.

Henry praised his lovely daughter, referred to the long wait she had had to finally marry her 'Mr Right' and made the usual remark about not losing a daughter but gaining another son. He went on to say that, once he was fully retired, he and Eliza planned to take a sea voyage to Malaya and spend a few weeks there with Joss and Gladys. This was news to Joss, but he welcomed it, guessing that Gladys would miss her family more than she presently thought she would.

Joss confined himself to raising a toast to his beautiful bride, complimenting the bridesmaids, and thanking Henry for providing them with this wonderful reception.

After they had cut the cake, Gladys suddenly remembered she had not yet thrown her bouquet.

"Line up behind me, ladies!" she called out.

She had tried to aim at Theresa's spinster sisters, Sarah and Edith, but it was Mabel who actually caught it. Her brothers hooted with laughter.

"Who's going to marry you?!" Donald said.

"I expect they will be queuing up later on," Will said, "but not for a while yet!"

When the festivities were over, Gladys and Joss went back to the Healeys' so that Gladys could change. Joss found that all his things had already been moved over to her room, which was quite large and contained a double bed. When Gladys was out of the room, he quickly checked the contents of his trunk. They were undisturbed and the toys he had bought for Theo were still secreted at the bottom, well wrapped and underneath books and other innocuous items. Had they been found, he could always have said he had been asked to buy some things for friends who had a small child. The photographs of Theo would be harder to explain, but he had hidden those inside the lining of the trunk.

Gladys asked him to undo the buttons of her dress which fastened down the back. He did so, kissing the creamy skin thus exposed. He commented on the brassiere she was wearing, which he also recalled unfastening when they were up on the moors.

"They've only been available for a few years," she said. "Much more comfortable than corsets!"

Henry drove them to the station. He and Eliza had given them a wedding present of a five day honeymoon in one of the best hotels in Scarborough. They thanked him again as they said goodbye.

"Just have a good time!" he said, smiling. "I'm sure you will!"

Sitting close together on the train journey, both of them were on fire with pent up desire, anticipating the joy of finally being able to make love without any constraints. As soon as they were alone in their hotel room, they fell onto the bed, removing their clothes as fast as they could, desperate for the feel of their bare skin connecting. Joss pulled out the pins from her hair, letting it cascade down her back, and ran his fingers through the glossy dark strands.

"What have I done to deserve such a lovely lady for my wife?"

The honeymoon passed all too swiftly, in a blur of happiness. Scarborough had been the object of a German naval bombardment during the first winter of the war and some evidence of this remained, but the town still retained much of its former elegance. The Crown hotel, where they were staying, had survived intact, although it was suffering wartime restrictions in staffing and supplies. Nevertheless, the service was impeccable, the food the best it could be and dances were still held regularly. Gladys relished being addressed as Mrs. Goldthorp by the staff, her married name still being a novelty. Guests dressed for dinner and she had brought some of her best evening gowns with her. Escorting her into the dining room and partnering her on the dance floor, Joss was convinced she was the most beautiful woman there. In the daytime, after breakfasting in bed and rising late, they wandered around the town, hand in hand, sampling the sights and activities. It was not warm enough to swim, but the weather remained mostly dry. When the cold wind hit them as they walked along the promenade, it served as an excuse to cuddle close for warmth. They found themselves constantly wanting to touch one another and would reach for each other's hands under the table in cafes and at dinner. They made love night and morning and sometimes returned to their room in the afternoon.

"I didn't think it was possible to love you any more," Gladys said, towards the end of their stay, "but I do. My feelings have grown even stronger these last few days."

"Mine too. I feel incredibly close to you - as if our souls have become entwined!"

Neither of them referred to the inevitable parting in less than one month's time, but both were very aware of it and the fact that they had been there before was of little consolation.

On the Saturday, which annoyingly was the first really warm day, they returned to Brighouse.

"No need to ask if you've had a good time," Henry said, smiling. "I can tell by your faces!"

When they were alone, Eliza asked her daughter if everything had been satisfactory 'in the bedroom department'.

"Everything was absolutely wonderful, Mother, and we couldn't get enough of each other!"

A day or two prior to the wedding, Eliza had taken Gladys aside and started to brief her on the physical side of marriage. Gladys had forestalled her, telling her she had heard all about such things in detail from her married friends, refraining from mentioning that she had also sampled them first hand.

The next day they went over to Heckmondwike. Joss and Will took a short walk while the Sunday roast was being prepared, Gladys opting to stay and help Theresa.

"As you look like a cat who's just polished off a large bowl of cream, I'm assuming that your honeymoon lived up to expectations!" Will said, grinning.

"More than! We had a marvellous time."

"Did you manage to get yourselves out of your hotel room for long enough to see something of Scarborough?"

"Yes, of course we did!"

They stayed a further week in Yorkshire, until the end of Gladys' holiday, returning on the following Sunday. The next morning, Joss rose early with Gladys so they could breakfast together and he then escorted her to work. He also met her in the evening and they walked back to Bedford Place. That pattern continued for the next few days until the Friday, when he travelled back up to Yorkshire to spend Friday night and part of Saturday in Heckmondwike. On his return, Gladys greeted him as though he had been away for weeks.

"I missed you last night," she said. "The bed was empty and cold without you. I suppose it was a taste of what's to come in ten days time. I've been trying not to think about it, but it's looming ever closer."

He wrapped his arms around her. "Hopefully, the war will be over in a few more months and then you can join me."

The following Thursday evening, Joss took Lavinia and Gladys out to the theatre and to supper afterwards. It was by way of thanks to Lavinia for her hospitality. Later, as they were getting ready for bed, he told Gladys he wanted to spend his last weekend in England up in Yorkshire with his family.

"I won't see any of them again for five years."

She was silent for a minute then said: "But it's our last weekend together too."

"I know, darling, and I don't want to be away from you any longer than necessary. Can't you come up to Yorkshire after work on Saturday?"

"Yes, I suppose so." She would have preferred to have him to herself that last weekend, but understood his wish to spend a final couple of days with Will and the children. "Are you going up tomorrow?"

"Yes." He came over to her where she was sitting at the dressing table and nuzzled the back of her neck. "Don't be upset, sweetheart, we'll only be apart for one night."

Her composure suddenly deserted her and her eyes filled with tears. "We're going to be apart for months or even longer as from Tuesday! Every little bit of time together is precious!"

She turned to face him. "Couldn't you ask for another six months leave on half pay? You're entitled to that, aren't you? Can't you send them a telegram saying you're unable to come back yet?"

He was startled. "No, I can't do that!"

"Why not?"

He patiently explained. "For one thing, it would mean someone else was unable to take leave, and that's hardly fair. For another, I'd be in danger of being sacked and at the very least I'd have scuppered my chances of promotion. I could kiss goodbye to any chance of ever becoming a Resident - or you a Resident's wife." He added lightly: "Surely you'd like to be the queen of a Malay State? I can just see you in that role!"

"Right now, I don't much care about that, but I'm sorry, I shouldn't have asked that of you." She stood and put her arms round his neck. "I just love you so very much and I need you, especially now."

"What do you mean, especially now?"

She hesitated. "I wasn't going to say anything because it may well be a false alarm and I don't want to get your hopes up, but I'm a few days late - and that's never happened before."

It took him a few seconds to comprehend her meaning. "You're going to have a baby?!"

"I might be, but it's very early days - oh, I shouldn't have said anything, it's too soon!"

"Yes, you should! This is wonderful news! Oh, my darling, my dearest love!" He clasped her to him.

87

"I might be wrong," she warned. "Please don't be too disappointed if I am. But there have been one or two other signs. I've been feeling quite tired this last week or so and my breasts feel tender, and I remember one of my friends saying that's how she felt right at the very beginning before she even knew she was expecting. And she said she became more emotional too - and I've just demonstrated that, haven't I!"

A little later, as they lay in bed, he said: "Perhaps I shouldn't go up until Saturday evening. I could travel up with you."

"No, you want to spend more time than that with them. I was being silly and selfish. You go tomorrow and I'll join you Saturday evening."

Joss spent Friday and Saturday on tenterhooks. Gladys had asked him not to say anything to anyone there before she arrived and they were a bit more certain.

"By Sunday morning, I'll be one week late; let's wait until then."

He had an enjoyable time playing games with the children on Saturday and Will joined them in the afternoon having again taken time off from the shop. They played football with the boys in the garden for a while then left them to it and sat on the bench, chatting.

"How do you feel about going back?" Will asked. "Or is that a daft question?"

"Much the same as last time. It's going to be a wrench to leave you all and heartbreaking to leave Gladys, although hopefully she'll be able to join me before too long."

"There are signs that this war might finally be drawing to a close," Will said. "It's been a senseless war from the start. So much loss of life, and for what? I know of several young men who have returned so badly injured that their lives will never be the same again and others who have no physical injuries but whose minds are shot to pieces."

"I have no idea what the situation is with my friends who are fighting. I suppose I won't know until the war ends and I hear from them - or I don't," Joss replied reflectively.

"I hope your ship doesn't come to any harm on the way over. I shall worry about that until I hear from you, so please write as soon as you land."

"Gladys has asked me to send her a telegram as soon as I land."

"That's a good idea. Ask her to let us know that you're safe."

Returning to Brighouse after tea, Joss borrowed Henry's car to meet Gladys off her train. Driving back, he started to ask the question uppermost on his mind. She interrupted before he finished.

"Yes, I'm still late, and I'm still feeling the same. We'll just give it until tomorrow morning. You haven't let anything slip, have you?"

"No, but it was hard! I was bursting to tell Will. It's a wonder he didn't guess something was up; he can often read me like a book!"

The situation was unchanged the next morning. Gladys told her mother first, when they were alone in the kitchen, getting breakfast. Mary Ellen's replacement always had Sundays off. Eliza was delighted and told her that she had had exactly the same early symptoms with all her pregnancies.

"With Frank I didn't at first realise what it meant, but with you and Alice I knew straight away. I'm so happy for you, love, it's wonderful news!"

They relayed the news to Henry over breakfast. He beamed from ear to ear, kissed his daughter and shook Joss' hand heartily.

At Heckmondwike, they waited until they had Will and Theresa alone, the children being out in the garden. They were effusive with their congratulations and Theresa started to give Gladys advice. Will grasped Joss by the shoulder and steered him out into the garden.

"Let the women talk female stuff together!" he said. "I'm really happy for you. I know how much you've wanted this."

"It's going to make leaving her even more painful. I'll be leaving our baby too. She wanted me to send a telegram to the FMS saying I'm taking another six months leave, but of course I can't do that."

"Do you have any idea what job you'll be returning to?"

"No. I'm hoping for an acting or assistant Resident's position, but that's probably pie in the sky."

"Why?"

"Because of my background. The colonial service is still a very conservative organisation."

Will was silent for a moment, then said, speaking slowly. "You know, in the aftermath of this war, we might well see a speeding up of the changes already starting to take place in our society. The right to vote has now been extended to all men and some women and this may well accelerate the erosion of the class system in time. We won't be having a revolution like the Russians, but I wouldn't be surprised if within our lifetimes we get to a stage where all men are judged solely on merit."

"You may well be right but it will probably come too late for my career. I can claim a pension at age fifty-five and that's only seventeen years off."

"Will you return to England then?"

"I expect so."

"Good! It'll be nice not to have you thousands of miles away most of the time."

When the children were told that, all being well, they would have a new cousin next year, Mabel put in a request for it to be a girl.

"There are far too many boys in this family!"

At the end of the day, they tried not to prolong the goodbyes. Joss and Gladys had driven over in Henry's car and the family all gathered outside to see them off. Back in Brighouse, they collected their things, Joss bade farewell to Eliza, then Henry drove them to the station.

On the train, Joss asked Gladys whether she was going to continue to work at the war office.

"Yes, of course. I don't need to leave yet. It's not a physical job - I sit in an office all day - and at Lavinia's house I'm thoroughly pampered, with all her servants."

"I suppose that's true. But if you start to find it too much, you must give in your notice and go back home. Promise me!"

"Yes, I promise. I want this baby as much - possibly even more - than you do and I'm not going to do anything which might jeopardise its safe delivery. You can rest assured of that."

"You should go to see a doctor too."

"Yes, I will, in a few weeks time when they'll be able to confirm it."

"I'll leave you some money. Doctors are not cheap, especially in London."

"No need, darling. I've plenty of money. Aunt Lavinia will only accept a pittance from me for my keep so I've been saving quite a lot from my wages. I have a very healthy bank balance!"

"Even so, you're my wife now and I should support you. Once I get back, I'll start sending you money regularly."

"There's no point. Save it to spend on me and the baby when we get there. If I do need money, I'll let you know, but I can't see that happening."

Joss was not sure whether to be glad about this or not. His male pride made him want to be the breadwinner, but not having to send money to England would be helpful, bearing in mind he also had Theo to support.

Back in London, they told Lavinia their news and she also congratulated them warmly. When Gladys was upstairs, Joss asked Lavinia whether she would be at home on Tuesday when Gladys returned from seeing him off (she was taking the day's leave she had left from the Whitsun weekend).

"I think she may need some support."

"Yes, don't worry, I'll look after her. And I'll refer her to my doctor. Bearing in mind that she's rather older than average for a first-time mother, I think it would be a good idea for her to be under medical supervision throughout her term."

Joss was happy to agree with that.

The remaining hours sped by and Tuesday morning dawned. Neither of them could eat much breakfast. Joss finished packing his case - his trunk had been sent to Tilbury earlier direct from Brighouse - then waited for Gladys to be ready. She was tense and snapped at him when he tried gently to hurry her up.

"We've plenty of time!"

She was ready a few minutes later and they set off. On the way to the station, she apologised for speaking sharply.

"Our last few hours together should be as perfect as we can make them."

"We're both wound up. We can't pretend to be happy when we're not."

"You always seem to manage to be calm!"

"I may be a bit less volatile than you, but I have my moments - as you'll find out when we're living together permanently!"

"Yes, I know we've both still got a lot to learn about each other, but I can't wait to start!"

"Me neither." Then he voiced something which had not yet been discussed between them. "If the war goes on until the end of this year - or even longer, heaven forbid - then it may be too near your time to risk a sea voyage and you may have to wait until after the baby is born."

"I know. I have thought of that. I'll take medical advice and do whatever they recommend. We can't take any risks with this baby. It may be our last chance to be parents."

At Tilbury, the scene was more or less a replay of 1911, and they both found it just as harrowing. He left it until the last minute to embark but still had to leave her crying bitterly on the dock. By the time he made it up onto the deck, he was relieved to see that she had recovered some degree of composure and she managed a watery smile and a wave.

When the ship had disappeared out to sea and she could no longer see him, she turned and, with a heavy heart, made her way back to the station. When the train arrived, she settled herself into a carriage, placing a hand protectively on her belly. She was once again returning to a life without the man she loved so deeply, but this time she had a new life inside her to be nurtured and she must focus all her energy on bringing a healthy baby into the world.

End of Part II

Part III

Chapter 8

Joss docked at Singapore in early September. He took a local steamer up the coast to Kuala Lumpur, and arrived in the midst of one of the torrential downpours which were such a feature of the country. When he reported for duty, he was told he would be taking over as District Officer in Raub, in Pahang State, with effect from 1st November, but meanwhile would be based at the secretariat in the capital.

He had served in Raub as Assistant D.O. during his first tour of duty and therefore knew it well. It was a gold mining district. The European population was quite small, but the town nevertheless had a clubhouse and was a pleasant enough place to be based. The District Officer's house was an imposing residence, which would please Gladys. The only problem was that it lay on the far side of the mountains and some considerable distance from Klang and Theo.

On the Saturday afternoon following his return, he set off for Klang, armed with the presents he had bought for Theo in England. Arriving at Alya's family home, her mother told him she was no longer living there.

"She's back in your old house. She's living with the new *Tuan*, and she's having another baby. He says he's going to marry her." She spoke in a matter of fact manner, but Joss imagined he heard a note of reproach; this man was going to do right by her daughter, unlike Joss.

Unsure whether this was good or bad news as far as Theo's welfare was concerned, he made his way over to his former home. It would be beneficial for the child's English language skills to be living with an Englishman, but might he be treated as a second class citizen in the family once their own child was born?

Alya let him in. Her pregnancy must be in the very early stages, he thought, as she was not showing yet.

"Your mother told me that you're having a baby and you are to be married."

She nodded.

"Congratulations. But what about Theo?"

"Theo lives here with us. He calls Jim 'Uncle' and they get on well. You have no need to worry."

The subject of their conversation ran into the room. He had grown, Joss thought; he looked like a proper little boy now, no longer a toddler. He stopped short when he saw Joss.

"Look who's here!" Alya said. "Daddy - back from England."

The child hung back shyly at first but Joss continued to talk to him and held up one of the gifts he had brought - a model of a London bus. Theo's eyes lit up and he came over to Joss, reaching out for the toy.

"Don't I get a kiss?"

Theo obliged and then did not pull away when Joss hugged him.

"It might take a little while until he's used to you again," Alya said. "It's over eight months since he's seen you and that's a long time in his short life."

"Yes, I know. I expected this. I've been missing him but he's probably forgotten all about me."

"No, he hasn't. When your cards came, he smiled and said 'from Daddy!' For a while, he kept asking when you were coming again."

Joss gave him the other toys he had brought and they watched him playing happily.

"Where are you based now?" Alya asked.

"Kuala Lumpur, but only until the end of October, then I take over as D.O. in Raub."

"That's a long way from here."

"Yes, I know.   It's going to make visiting Theo difficult, especially once Gladys gets here."

"I suppose she can't come until the war ends?"

"Maybe even later. She's having a baby."

It was Alya's turn to congratulate him.

Jim arrived home. He was a man in his mid forties and looked familiar to Joss.

"We've met, haven't we?" Jim said, as they shook hands. "Way back, before the war, at the Selangor club?"

"Yes, I think so."

"I thought the name was familiar, when Alya told me who Theo's father was." He turned to greet Theo, who was showing him his new toys. "He's a grand little fellow. We're having our own baby now, as I expect Alya's told you, but you needn't worry that I'll treat Theo any differently."

Alya left the room, and the two men fell into general conversation, Jim asking about life in England in wartime.

"I'll be retiring back there in about 10 years time," he said, "and of course Theo can come with us, unless you want to make other arrangements for him. Do your family in England know about him?"

Joss shook his head. "No, and neither does my wife. Perhaps, after our baby is born and she's settled in here, I'll eventually dare to tell her!"

"Difficult one, that. She might turn tail and go back to England! Where are you based now?"

Joss told him. "Once I'm in Raub, it will be a long journey to Klang and back."

"Yes, and you won't want to drive on that winding mountain road after dark. I know, why don't you stay overnight here? Get here as early as you can on Saturday and leave after *tiffin* on Sunday. You can sleep in Theo's room; there's another bed in there."

"That's very good of you."

"Not at all. Mind you, once your wife gets here, you'll have to be quite inventive thinking up reasons for your absence on those weekends!"

As they continued to chat, Jim told Joss he wanted to stay in Klang, if possible, until his retirement, and had put in an official request to that effect.

"At least, I want to stay as a D.O. I don't want to be transferred back to one of the main towns. I've had enough of desk jobs; I like the variety of working in the Districts. It will also make it easier being married to a native girl."

Until his departure to Raub, Joss visited Theo every weekend and their relationship was soon back on track. On the last visit before his transfer, he explained to him that he would probably not be able to come to see him each weekend in future, as he would be living much further away, but when he did come he would be staying the night and sleeping in his room, so they would have more time together. Theo seemed to accept this quite happily.

In Raub, Joss' Assistant D.O. was an affable young man in his twenties called Arthur. After he had been there about a week and they had got to know each other, Joss broached the subject of his planned trips to Klang, every second or third weekend.

"So, I'll need to leave you in charge, in case anything urgent crops up here out of hours, and I'll also need to take the car - unless you don't mind driving me over the mountains to Kuala Kubu, where I can get the train? You'd then need to pick me up there on the Sunday."

Arthur said he did not mind being left in charge. "It will give me the chance to take on more responsibility and gain experience. But, if anyone asks why you are away, what shall I say?"

Joss debated whether to tell him the truth, then decided that he really had no option; he needed his co-operation.

"It depends on who's asking! If the Resident of Pahang or his staff enquire, I'd rather you were vague about it, but the truth is that

I'm going to visit my small son." He briefly summarised the situation with Alya and Theo.

Arthur raised an eyebrow. "Right; I'd heard about chaps taking Asian mistresses but I've never met one before! What about your wife, when she finally arrives? Does she know?"

"No, she doesn't. And I'll need it to stay that way, at least at first, until she's settled and happy here. Then I might eventually confess my sins and thrown myself on her mercy!"

"What if she then insists you stop seeing your son?"

Joss had not thought of that. "I'll have to hope that she doesn't! She's not a vindictive person and she has quite liberal and tolerant views in general. Hopefully, they'll extend to my situation, once she's got over the initial shock!"

"Until you do tell her, how will you explain your absences?"

"I don't know! I haven't thought that far ahead. I'll have to make them less frequent and perhaps sometimes go during the working week instead of at weekends - in which case I'd need you to support whatever story I tell her and also cover for me at work. I'm sorry, I know it's asking an awful lot!"

"I don't really mind - I suppose we chaps have to stick together! You'll owe me one though!"

~ * ~

Meanwhile, back in England, Gladys, blissfully unaware of Theo's existence, was concentrating on her own, as yet unborn child. She had been to see the doctor, who had confirmed that her baby was due at the end of March. He was monitoring her carefully, at not inconsiderable cost. She had anxiously awaited Joss' telegram, advising of his safe landing in Singapore, and, once it had arrived, had asked Lavinia to telephone William at his shop the next day, as she was not allowed to use the war office telephones for personal calls. Will and Theresa did not yet have a telephone installed at home; Henry and Eliza had only quite recently acquired one.

When she started to experience morning sickness, it caused her to be late for work on several occasions and she was called in to the manager's office to explain herself. When she told him the reason, he suggested she give in her notice and 'concentrate on her domestic duties'.

"I don't have any domestic duties. My husband is out in Malaya and I'm living in a house full of servants."

"Hmm, well, when the war finally comes to an end - which won't be long now - the men will start returning and, of course, all those who want their jobs back will get them. Therefore I shall have to lay off many of you women. Bearing in mind your condition, you'll be one of the first to go, I'm afraid."

On Armistice day, there was widespread jubilation all over the country, and the streets of London were crowded with people celebrating. The staff at the war office downed tools for the rest of the day and held a party. When she eventually left to head home, Gladys found she had to fight her way through throngs of revellers. She would have liked to join them, but was afraid for the well-being of her baby and eventually took to the side streets to try to avoid being further jostled. She was not yet heavily enough pregnant for it to be obvious through a winter coat, so no particular consideration would be shown to her. She was also rather afraid of catching the dreaded Spanish flu, in such close proximity to crowds of people.

She contacted the colonial office about a passage to Malaya, but was told that it would be some time before the requisitioned ships would be refitted and returned to normal service and the earliest passage they could offer her was in mid February. As this was far too near to the due date of her baby - she risked giving birth on the ship - she declined the offer, explaining the reason, and asked to be given a date in late May. She was told to contact them again after the birth.

As her job would soon be over anyway, she decided to call it a day and return home to await the birth of her child up in Yorkshire. She handed in her notice and telephoned her parents.

~ * ~

In Malaya, celebrations were also taking place everywhere. The club house in Raub was more festively decorated than at Christmas and the bar was doing a roaring trade on Armistice day evening. Joss was drinking *stengahs* with Arthur, a couple of the gold miners, and the Resident of Pahang and his assistant. One of the miners commented that the loss of so many young men was hardly something to be celebrated.

"We're celebrating the fact that it's over, " Arthur said. "No more will die."

"Until the next time," the other miner responded.

Joss was inclined to share their cynicism. He recalled how Will Stocks' first action upon returning home on leave had been to take a very long, hot bath, 'to scrub the blood and filth of the trenches off me.' Joss had shared a bedroom with him for two nights prior to the wedding and had heard him muttering and groaning in his sleep, although, when asked about his experiences, he had said very little. He hoped that Will had survived the war and that he, and all the other men he knew who had been fighting, would now return home safely.

As he settled into life in Raub, Joss found he relished being back in a rural area, after two years spent in the capital. There was a sense of freedom in leaving the office and taking the car out to remote areas of the district, to arbitrate in land disputes or deal with issues at the mines. He had always appreciated the wild beauty of the jungle and he enjoyed his scenic drives over the hills to visit Theo, despite the hairpin bends which required him to have all his wits about him.

As he left the simmering heat of the valley behind, and climbed up into the mountains, there was a peace and serenity in being alone on the road, although it was frustrating to have his speed slow to 10 mph or less. Even when he ceased ascending, he dare not pick up much speed as he still had to navigate the bends. As a result, the total journey took about four and a half hours each way. Despite this, he made the trip every second or third weekend.

Theo would be expecting him and would run outside as soon as he heard the car. Being there overnight meant Joss could put Theo to bed and read him a story and, early the following morning, he would be awakened by the child climbing onto his bed. In the late evenings, he and Jim played cards or chess and sometimes visited the club. Having previously lived in Klang, he knew many of the Europeans who frequented it and it was not long before one of the planters asked him why he visited Klang so often.

"It's quite a trek over from Raub."

Joss explained, and the man chuckled. "So, you've both sampled the same lady and your children will be half-siblings! It's good that you're able to be friends."

"No reason why we shouldn't be," Jim replied. "Joss' relationship with Alya was over long before I met her."

"Very modern!" the other man observed. Then, turning to Joss: "What happened to your English fiancee?"

"She's now my wife."

"But she's still in England?"

"Yes. We're having a baby and she wasn't able to get a passage straight after the war ended so she will now have to wait until after it's born."

"But what the hell are you going to do about your situation once she gets here? I assume she doesn't know?"

Joss was getting rather tired of being asked this, especially as he still had no idea himself. He merely shrugged. At that point, the two men's wives came up to them and the subject was dropped. He hoped that his predicament would not be relayed to the women later, as it might then become the subject of gossip which could one day reach Gladys' ears.

As they walked home, Jim returned to the same theme.

"I take it you still haven't worked out an excuse to account for your visits?"

"Not really, but time is on my side. She won't be arriving until the summer now. I may even be moved somewhere else by then, hopefully nearer to Klang."

Jim laughed. "Or they may send you somewhere further away! You'd better hope that they don't transfer you to Brunei!"

On his journey back to Raub the next day, Joss found his thoughts returning to that conversation. He certainly hoped he would not be sent to Brunei. So far, his posts had all been within the FMS, but transfers further afield were a possibility. If he were to be merely a D.O. there, he could request to be sent elsewhere, citing his newly arrived wife and young baby as a reason, but if he were offered an Acting Resident position and he turned that down, the chance might never arise again. Being several days sea journey away, visiting Theo from Brunei would only be possible during his annual local leave. He knew that Theo would always be well looked after by Jim and Alya, but he would miss him dreadfully and their relationship would suffer. He would become a semi stranger to his son. Still, such a posting would not go on forever - a year or so later he would be back in the FMS.

A more pressing problem still had to be faced. When he had received Gladys' telegram, telling him she was unable to sail until after the birth, he had been very disappointed. He was missing her even more this time than last, and he also wanted to see and hold his new son or daughter straight away. However, the delay had granted him a short reprieve; until she arrived, he could continue spending his regular weekends with Theo. He had still not decided what to do after that. The risk of her returning to England and taking their child

102

with her, or insisting he sever all relations with Theo, made him reluctant to tell her the truth, but the logistics of managing to see Theo without her finding out, especially when still in Raub, were daunting, to say the least. 'What a pickle I've landed myself in,' he thought. 'I've often criticised my brother for taking the moral high ground on issues, but if I'd been more like him and turned down the chance to live with Alya, I wouldn't be in this mess now. The first really significant moral dilemma of my life and I failed it miserably! But how can I wish that Theo hadn't been born?!'

As he started the ascent into the mountains, he stopped churning everything over in his mind and concentrated on the road. If he were to misjudge one of the bends and plunge down the hillside, his problems would probably be over for good! Arriving back in Raub, and driving past the colourful Chinese temple, another thought struck him. He should take some precautions regarding Theo in case anything did happen to him. After their wedding, he and Gladys had made wills leaving everything to each other and appointing each other as executors. This would mean that his belongings would be packed up and sent to her. He needed to put the copy of Theo's birth certificate and the photos of him into a sealed packet, addressed to his brother, so they reached him instead. He would enclose a letter, telling Will everything and asking him to acknowledge his nephew, but without telling Gladys. He should also start transferring money into a separate bank account in Alya's name, for Theo's education, and leave a sealed note for her about that. He resolved to address both issues as soon as possible.

In the early New Year, Joss heard from Will that Crossland and Ewart had both survived the war and were shortly to be demobbed. He had similar good news from Gladys regarding Will Stocks. He wrote to those of his friends who had been fighting and hoped he would soon hear from them. Will's next letter told him that the family had acquired a dog at Christmas, a large shaggy crossbreed, and that Ewart was being as good as his word in walking him before school each morning. Joss imagined a large dog in that already rather crowded household and felt quite glad that he would be based at the Healeys' more spacious home during his future leaves.

~ * ~

Chapter 9

Meanwhile, Gladys was preparing for the arrival of her baby. The pram and cot, last used for her sister Alice, had been retrieved from the attic and she and Eliza were busy knitting and sewing baby clothes. By February, she was in the seventh month of her term. She felt heavy and tired and was suffering many of the minor ailments common in pregnancy.

"It's just as well that Joss is not here to see me," she said to Eliza. "I look like a beached whale!"

"Don't be silly! You're carrying his baby. He'd still think you're beautiful."

The influenza epidemic, referred to as the Spanish Flu, which had claimed many lives during 1918, was thought to have run the worst of its course by the end of the year. It had mainly affected younger adults and pregnant women were at increased risk of infection, so Eliza and Henry were very relieved when Gladys left London, which they regarded as a hotbed of infection. It was true that the south of England had been far harder hit by the first two waves of the epidemic, but when a third wave commenced in the early New Year, this time it was the turn of the north of the country.

Despite taking every precaution and rarely venturing into the town, Gladys somehow became infected. One evening in February, she started complaining of extreme fatigue, severe headache and aching limbs, and went to bed very early. By the early hours of the morning, she was seriously ill, with a racking cough, high fever and a throat which felt as if she were swallowing knives. These symptoms escalated rapidly; her coughing became so violent it was feared she would tear her abdominal muscles, as many did, and her fever reached 104 degrees. Vomiting and diarrhoea set in and she was frequently struggling for breath, her skin taking on a blue tinge as a result of the reduced oxygen levels. From time to time her nose bled copiously.

The doctor was summoned, who prescribed quinine and codeine, but warned that they would have only minimal effect and the disease would have to run its course. He did not need to tell her distraught parents that this may well end with her death from pneumonia.

No-one could have had a more devoted nurse than Eliza. She stayed with her daughter day and night, just snatching brief catnaps in a chair by her bedside. She ministered to her every need; cleaning up blood, vomit and other bodily excretions, sponging her with cool water to try to bring down the fever, coaxing her to take drinks. Their maid, Annie, and her daughter-in-law, Mary, both offered to relieve her vigil so that she could get some rest but she refused.

"You are both young; you're in the age group most susceptible to this dreadful disease. I can't let you risk it. I'm old; it won't get to me."

Henry sent off a telegram to Joss, letting him know that Gladys was dangerously ill. He knew that his son-in-law could do nothing but worry, thousands of miles away, but felt he did not have the right to keep the situation from him. Henry himself prayed morning and night.

"Please, God, in your mercy, let her recover. Please don't take her from us. You already have one of our daughters - let that be enough."

Gladys was frequently delirious, seemingly unaware of her surroundings, and periodically calling out Joss' name. In her lucid spells, she begged Eliza not to let her lose her baby. She reverted to calling Eliza 'Mummy', a term she had not used since she was about twelve, and Eliza's heart contracted.

After four or five days, Henry insisted on his wife getting some proper rest.

"I'll sit with her for a while."

"But she may need something doing for her which a man can't do."

"Then I'll call you. Right now, she seems to be sleeping. Get some sleep while you can, Eliza, or you'll become ill too."

After just over a week, she started to slowly recover. The fever subsided, the coughing fits became less violent, the vomiting, diarrhoea and bleeding gradually reduced and eventually ceased. She was still ill and extremely weak, but it looked as though her life had been spared. The doctor came again and pronounced that the worst was over.

"She should recover now. It will take several weeks before she feels herself again and the cough will probably linger; she must get plenty of rest."

"What about the baby, Doctor?" Eliza asked anxiously. "Is everything all right?"

"Seems to be. She's a lucky lady."

Henry and Eliza both gave thanks to God for sparing her, and Henry sent another telegram to Joss with the good news.

Gladys' fortieth birthday had been and gone while she was in the throes of the acute stage of her illness. The day after the doctor's visit, her parents gave her their card and present and also Joss', which had arrived the day she fell ill. There was also a gift from Frank and Mary and cards from various friends, Aunt Lavinia, and Will and Theresa. The doctor had advised against younger people visiting her for another week or so, in case she was still infectious, but Henry contacted everyone with a telephone to let them know she had turned the corner and was on the road to recovery.

Joss had given her a beautiful necklace, in an unusual design. Eliza, admiring it, commented:

"I expect there's a lot of interesting jewellery in the shops out there. Once you're living there, I shall expect some exotic Christmas and birthday presents from you!"

Gladys managed a smile. She had now started to drink the nourishing broths which Annie prepared for her and had even managed a small amount of solid food.

"We need to fatten you up again!" Henry said. "If it wasn't for your baby belly, you'd be as thin as a rake!"

"Yes, and you also need to feed the baby," Eliza added.

Reaching out and clasping her mother's hand, Gladys said earnestly.

"Thank you for looking after me so well, Mother. I daresay it's mainly due to your nursing care that I've come through this. I probably owe you my life!"

"I could have done nothing else. However old you become, you are still my child."

Several days later, Henry was sitting reading to Gladys, who still found it tiring to hold a book for long. She was enjoying listening to the story unfold and feeling relaxed and peaceful, until a sudden pain in her abdomen caused her to gasp. Henry stopped reading and looked at her questioningly.

"I think the baby might be starting!"

"I'll get your mother."

By the time Eliza entered the room, she had felt several more contractions.

"Oh, no, it can't come yet! It's too early. It's not due for another month!"

"It might be a false alarm - I had that with one of you three - but if it is the real thing, babies born a month early can still live. Try not to panic!"

Her contractions continued over the next hour or two, becoming more frequent, and then she felt a warm flood between her legs. Aghast, she wailed:

"I'm all wet!"

"Your waters have broken then. So labour has definitely started."

Eliza called downstairs for Henry to telephone the midwife and for Annie to bring up hot water and towels.

Gladys' labour continued over the next six or seven hours. When the contractions came hard and fast and she could hardly bear the pain, she screamed out loud and squeezed Eliza's hand hard.

"You never told me it was this awful!" she sobbed.

"I suppose you forget. It's actually quicker and easier with later births; the first one is the worst."

" Right now, that's not much help!"

Knowing that a first labour would probably take several hours, the midwife had not rushed to get there. An hour or two after she arrived, she announced that the baby's head could now be seen.

"Push now, when I tell you to!" she ordered. She was a brisk, no-nonsense, middle aged woman.

Gladys, still very weak from the flu, soon became utterly exhausted.

"I can't push any more, I can't!"

"Yes, you can," Eliza said soothingly. "You have to - the baby has to come out!"

"Right, the head's nearly out. Stop pushing for a few minutes. "

The midwife held the baby's head as it emerged into the world.

"Now, one last big push!"

Gladys made what felt like a superhuman effort, yelling at the top of her voice, and the baby's body slithered out.

"There now, you've got a baby girl! And she's not a bad size for an eight month term."

Gladys felt a rush of joy, mixed with relief that her ordeal was over.

"Can I hold her?"

"Just a minute; I'm cutting the cord."

A strange silence followed. The midwife looked properly at the baby girl, who was making no sound. She tried to stimulate her, but to no avail. A cold fear took hold of Eliza.

"Why isn't she crying?"

The midwife eventually gave up trying to resuscitate the tiny body.

"I think this baby must have been dead inside her for several days."

Gladys let out a howl of pure anguish. "No! No! She can't be dead. Do something! Oh God, please do something!"

"I'm so sorry; there's nothing more I can do."

"Get the doctor then!"

"There'll be nothing he can do either. I'm very sorry dear, but your baby has been born dead. It'll be the flu that killed her."

Eliza, ashen-faced, tried to comfort Gladys. She pushed her away.

"I want my baby! I want to hold her!"

"There's no point; it will only make it worse for you," the woman answered.

"Give me my baby!"

Her voice rose on a crescendo, and Eliza took the baby from where the midwife had laid her and put the lifeless little body into Gladys' arms. She stroked the perfect, still little face and felt the tiny fingers and toes.

"She can't be dead! She can't be!"

She rubbed the baby's chest, trying desperately to instil life into the tiny body. Eliza watched her helplessly, tears rolling down her face.

The midwife finished delivering the placenta and, having cleaned Gladys up, stood up to leave. She reached for the baby and plucked her from Gladys' arms.

"No! No! Don't take her away; where are you going with her?"

She left the room without replying.

Gladys clutched Eliza's arm.

"Stop her! Don't let her take my baby!"

"My love, she's dead. There's nothing can be done. I'm so very sorry...."

"But don't let her take her away! We have to give her a proper funeral. We can bury her with Alice."

Eliza ran out of the room and started down the stairs. Henry was in the hall, looking stricken.

"Has she gone? Go after her, please. Get the baby back so we can bury her with Alice."

Henry ran down the path as fast as he could but when he reached the road, there was no sign of the woman and no way of knowing which way she had gone. He returned indoors and called up to Eliza:

"I was too late, but I'll telephone the doctor."

Eliza helped Gladys to wash and change into a clean nightdress. She brushed the tangles out of her hair and changed the bed linen. Throughout it all, Gladys wept softly. Grief clawed at her chest. She felt herself slipping beneath the surface of life into a dark abyss. The image of her daughter's tiny, still face swam before her eyes. She was aware of her full and heavy breasts, and longed to feel her baby suckle. What had she felt, inside the womb, before the life drained out of her? Had she felt pain? She looked across the room at the cot with its pretty bedclothes, where her baby should now be sleeping, and her heart felt ripped to shreds.

Henry spoke to the doctor, but was told that all the stillbirths that day would be delivered to the hospital and they would either be buried all together in an unmarked grave in non-consecrated ground, or sometimes the small bodies might be placed in the coffins of unrelated adults being interred that day.

"No-one would be able to tell now which baby was your grandchild, and you probably wouldn't be allowed to bury her in your other daughter's grave as the baby hasn't been baptised. The best thing you can do is persuade your daughter to return to her husband in Malaya as soon as she is well enough to travel and conceive another baby as soon as possible."

111

Henry went upstairs and knocked on Gladys' bedroom door. When Eliza came out, he shook his head in response to her questioning look.

"It's no good, he can't help."

He relayed the gist of the doctor's words, somewhat modified to soften the blow and leaving out his final comment.

"How could she have been baptised, when she was already dead? Even if we had had a minister standing by, it couldn't have been done!" Eliza said bitterly.

They both went into the room and gently explained the situation to Gladys.

"I'm so terribly sorry," Henry said, "but it was only her body; her soul has gone to heaven and she will be with Alice."

Gladys looked at him with deadened eyes, but said nothing.

"You were going to call a girl Alicia, weren't you?" Eliza asked, stroking Gladys' hair gently.

"Yes, we'd decided on Alicia Martha Elise." Her tears welled up again.

"Well, why don't you still give her that first name and think of her as Alicia, and when you and Joss talk about her, you can call her that? She will live on in your hearts and minds so she should have a name."

Gladys nodded.

"Try to get some sleep now," Eliza said, bending to kiss her daughter. Henry also hugged her.

"My darling girl, I really am so dreadfully sorry."

"I need to send Joss another telegram," Henry said as they left the room. "I'll phone everyone else tomorrow. And you need to get a good long rest." He looked at his wife; the last few weeks had taken their toll. "You're no longer young - neither of us are - and you need to recover too."

"She would have been our first grandchild," Eliza said sadly. They both thought of Frank and Mary who had not been blessed with a child. It was a source of sorrow to them but at least they had not had to go through this.

~ * ~

Meanwhile, in Raub, Joss received Henry's first telegram and read the words with mounting dread. Malaya had also had a flu epidemic and he knew many lives had been lost. 'Please God, don't let her die!' He spent the following nine days in a state of torment, unable to concentrate properly on his work, worry tying his guts in knots.

"I'm sure she'll pull through," Arthur said, in a vain attempt at dispensing comfort.

"How can you possibly know that?!" Joss snapped.

"Well, she'll be being well looked after, won't she?"

"That's no guarantee!"

When Henry's second telegram arrived, he hardly dared open it. His houseboy had brought it round to the office and he sat looking at it for a while, terrified it would tell him that Gladys was dead. His stomach churned and he felt sick. Eventually, Arthur took it from him and slit the envelope open.

"It's alright," he said, smiling, and patted Joss on the shoulder. "She's recovering! And the baby's alright too!"

"Oh, thank God!"

He read the words and felt tears of relief pricking the back of his eyelids. He abruptly left the room and went outside until he regained his composure. When he returned, Arthur suggested they have a celebratory drink at the club that evening.

That night, Joss wrote a long letter to Gladys, pouring out his love for her, the fear he had felt and his tremendous relief that she was recovering.

"......I don't know what I'd have done if I'd lost you; I don't think I could bear to carry on living without you. Even though we are *thousands of miles apart, at least I know you are in this world and we will be together before long....."*

The next morning, before going to the office, he called in to the protestant church and gave thanks to God for sparing the life of the woman he loved and their unborn child.

Henry's third telegram arrived almost exactly a week later, in early March. Joss was handed it as he arrived home that evening, having been out and about in the district all day. His houseboy hovered.

"I hope it's not bad news, *Tuan.*"

The servants were somehow always aware of what was going on and Haziq knew that the *Tuan*'s *Mem* in England had been very ill but was now getting better.

Joss opened the envelope with a pounding heart. He read the stark words:

"....born dead......a girl.....Gladys recovering.....so terribly sorry. Letter following. Henry."

The room swam and he had to sit down.

"Are you alright, *Tuan*?" Haziq asked.

"Just leave me, please."

His first thoughts were for Gladys, her suffering. She must be beside herself with grief. He needed to be there with her, helping her to get through this, giving her his love and support. They should be grieving together. If only he could talk to her! He pounded the arm of the chair in frustration. A girl! How he would have loved a little daughter! An image of Mabel at three years old sprang into his mind. What did their little girl look like? Had she been given a name? Where was she being buried? He supposed he would have to wait for Henry's letter to get the details.

He rose and paced the room, needing to be doing something but not knowing what. Darkness had fallen sometime ago, so going for a walk in the jungle was not an option, although it would have suited his mood. He thought about going to the club, but could not face having to talk to other people nor trust himself not to break down. He started to write to Gladys, trying to express his love and concern for her, but his own grief kept intruding and he did not want to burden her with that yet. Still, he had to let her know that he was grieving with her. He decided to send a telegram first, and write in a day or two. A letter took too long anyway; she needed to hear from him now. He wrote out a few well chosen words of love, support and sorrow and put it on the table for Haziq to send the next day. Then he poured himself a *stengah*.

Haziq knocked and put his head round the door. "What about dinner, *Tuan*?"

"I'm not hungry."

"You should eat something. Cook will make you something light."

Joss shrugged, not caring. "There's a return telegram there, to send in the morning, please."

Haziq took it. "Is it the *Mem* in England? Is she worse?"

Joss was tempted to tell him to mind his own business, but knew that he and the others would find out soon enough anyway. Besides, he normally treated the staff with respect and courtesy.

"It's our baby. It - she - has been born dead."

"I'm so sorry, *Tuan*, that is terrible!" There was genuine sympathy in his voice.

Joss managed a few mouthfuls of the light dish brought to him, and washed it down with further *stengah*s. He was tempted to finish the bottle, to seek oblivion, but he was not normally a heavy drinker and would probably just make himself sick. He retreated to the privacy of his bedroom and there allowed his grief full expression.

A couple of days later, yet another telegram arrived. Haziq brought it round to the office. Fear took hold of him again. What now? Had Gladys had a relapse? Was he still going to lose her, as well as their baby? This time he ripped it open quickly and then sagged with relief.

*"....Our thoughts are with you at this sad time....letter following.
Love Will and family."*

In response to Arthur's questioning look, he said. "It's just from
my brother. A sympathy telegram."

He read it again and thought that he would give a lot to have Will
here with him right now.

At the weekend, he set off for Klang. It was three weeks since he
had last seen Theo and he now longed to be with his son. Theo ran
out to the car, as he always did, and Joss picked him up and held him
close for a few moments. Alya greeted him; Jim was out
somewhere. Joss looked at Alya's swollen belly and remembered
with a jolt that her baby was due at around the same time as his and
Gladys' had been. He asked after her health.

"I'm well enough, but I'm looking forward to finally giving birth.
I expect your wife is feeling the same."

Sorrow washed over him again. His voice cracking, he said:

"Our baby has been stillborn. Gladys caught the flu; it didn't kill
her, thank God, but it killed our baby girl."

Alya's eyes widened. "I'm so very sorry!"

Any last remnants of jealousy she still felt for the woman who
had always owned Joss' heart melted away and she felt nothing but
sympathy for her - and for him. She put out her hand and clasped
his. Theo, watching them, asked:

"Why are you sad, Daddy?"

"Because a little baby in England has gone to heaven, to be with
Jesus and the angels."

Both England and heaven were only vague concepts to Theo. He
had been given a story book about the nativity at Christmas and he
wondered why it was a bad thing that this baby had gone to join
Jesus. Looking at his puzzled face, Joss ruffled his hair and told him
not to worry about it.

"You'll understand when you're a bit older." 'And then I'll tell
you that it was your half-sister', he thought.

Joss and Theo were kicking a ball around in the garden when Jim arrived home. He came outside to join them and delivered a well-aimed kick to the ball which sent it flying past Theo into the bushes at the far side. Theo turned and ran after it. Jim turned to Joss.

"Alya's just told me. I'm so very sorry, old chap. That's rotten luck."

"Thanks."

"I suppose you don't know yet when she'll be sailing?"

Joss shook his head. "She'll have to recover both from the flu and the birth. I hope it won't take too long; we need to be together."

Jim wisely refrained from commenting that this would make it even more difficult for Joss to tell Gladys about Theo. Now was not the time to labour that point.

~ * ~

Chapter 10

At night, Gladys dreamed about Alicia. She saw and felt her as a living, warm baby, then awoke to cold reality. She felt lost in a yawning cavern of emptiness. Empty arms, empty womb, empty heart. Henry had brought her pen and paper so that she could write to Joss, but so far she had left them untouched.

"I've lost his baby," she said to her father. "What can I say to him?"

"Share your grief with him. He'll be grieving too. He needs to hear from you."

Gladys looked at him with dull eyes. "No, he'll be disappointed, but he won't be feeling as I do. How can he? He never even saw her."

"That's not his fault, anymore than it's yours that she died. It's a tragedy for both of you and you need to communicate with each other. I'm sure a letter is on its way from him."

In fact, a letter had arrived a day or two after the birth, but of course it had been written before she fell ill. It was full of joyful anticipation about their baby's arrival and Gladys let it flutter to the floor, half unread.

Frank and Mary came to see her. Frank hugged his sister.

"I'm so terribly sorry, Glad."

Mary clasped her hand and told her how much she empathised with her loss.

"I thought it was bad enough being barren, but what has happened to you is far worse. I really feel for you, my dear."

Will Stocks arrived home, having been demobbed. Expecting an effusive welcome, he was dismayed to return to a house in mourning. Eliza embraced her nephew and told him how happy she was that he had returned safely, but he was shocked at her drawn, gaunt appearance. After she and Henry had told him what had happened, he went upstairs to see Gladys. His vivacious cousin had become another woman. The light had gone from her eyes, she was withdrawn and listless and seemed to have aged ten years since he had last seen her, as a glowing bride on her wedding day. He grasped her hand and kissed her cheek.

"Oh, Glad, I'm so very sorry! What can I say to you?"

"There's nothing anyone can say to make any difference, so don't try, Will. You've been to hell and back too, I know. I've read the reports of what our soldiers suffered at the front and I daresay they don't tell us the half of it."

"No, they don't. But never mind me. You need to concentrate on getting better, so you're well enough to travel to Malaya and be with Joss again."

"That's what everyone says, but I can't even think about that right now."

Henry had sent a letter to Joss a few days after the birth recounting the detail of the previous few weeks, but, when another couple of weeks had gone by without Gladys putting pen to paper, he sent a further letter, explaining Gladys' state of mind and that she did not yet feel able to write to him. He did not want to leave Joss without any communication, wondering why he was not hearing from his wife, although Will and Theresa were being kept informed and Will would doubtless be writing to his brother.

A couple of weeks after the birth, Gladys was well enough to leave her bed and come downstairs, for a few hours each day at first, gradually increasing. She started to slowly recover her physical health and put on some weight. Her milk eventually dried up and this eased the discomfort in her breasts. However, grief was still in charge of her heart and mind. She began going outside for short walks, at first just in the garden then venturing out into the street. There it seemed that women pushing prams were everywhere.

119

Sleeping babies, gurgling, smiling babies; each one she saw stabbed at her heart.

In mid April, two letters from Joss arrived in quick succession. The first one exulted in her recovery from the flu; the second had been written after he had heard of the baby's death. She absorbed his expressions of grief, his declarations of love, as if she were reading a book about other people. There was concern for her in every line, he desperately wished he could be with her, but it all left her unmoved. She could only focus on her dead baby. She knew she was being unfair and that she must reply to his letters, but she still put it off.

Theresa came to see her. She had to bring Stanley with her, but Eliza took him into the back room with her and left the two younger women alone. Theresa put her hand over Gladys'.

"I've never lost a child, but I think I can imagine how I would have felt if one of mine had been stillborn. I feel for you, my dear, I really do."

"Thanks."

"Will's had a letter from Joss. I expect you have too."

"Yes."

"He's heartbroken, and terribly concerned for you."

Gladys made no reply.

"I expect you think that he can't possibly be feeling as you do, and to a certain extent that's true. Men don't carry and give birth to babies. But they do still grieve when babies die."

"Perhaps, if he'd been here and seen her. But he's on the other side of the world. He never even saw me getting bigger, with her growing inside me, never put his hand on my tummy and felt her moving. The only part of her he's shared is her conception."

Theresa was silent for a moment, then said: "At least you are surrounded by a loving family. Joss is on his own out there. There's no-one he can really open up to. The sooner you are well enough to travel to Malaya, the better. You need to talk to each other.

Meanwhile, write and tell him how you feel; a marriage needs communication."

After she had gone, Gladys went upstairs, to find Henry in the process of dismantling the cot. She looked at him in dismay.

"There's no point in leaving it here," he said gently. "It's just a constant reminder of your loss."

When he had left the room, she opened the bottom drawer of the chest and looked at the piles of baby clothes, which would now never be worn. She fingered the tiny garments. Eliza came in as she was doing this, and also looked sadly at the little outfits she and Gladys had so lovingly knitted and sewed. Then she firmly shut the drawer. She sat down on the edge of the bed and indicated Gladys should join her.

"Don't do what I did after Alice died. I let my grief completely take me over; I sunk into it and let it possess me until the outside world ceased to exist. I had a husband and two other children who loved me but I let that count for nothing and just wallowed in my loss. You know - you witnessed it. Don't let that happen to you too."

"I'm trying not to, but I feel so hollow and drained. There's a hole in the midst of my soul where Alicia should be and no-one else can fill it."

"And no-one ever will. You'll never forget her, and I'm not saying you should. Grief never entirely goes away; it lurks inside you, waiting to catch you unawares. But time does heal eventually and having another baby will help the healing process."

"She can't just be replaced!"

"Of course not. But there's room in your heart, as in every woman's, to love more than one child, and loving and caring for another baby will help to take your mind off the one you have lost."

"I don't know if I can manage to conceive another baby - I'm forty now."

"You were thirty-nine last year and you managed it pretty quickly!"

"We were newly-weds and we gave it an awful lot of chances!"

"Well, when you and Joss are finally reunited, you can do that again."

"I'm not sure if I can feel the same. I still love him, underneath all this grief, but there's a barrier to my expressing it. That's why I can't write to him yet."

"But you must try. Just tell him how you feel, as you have told me; write from your heart. Think about how he'll be feeling, not hearing from you."

Gladys was reminded of Theresa's comment about Joss being on his own with his grief, with no-one he could really talk to, and a flash of the love she still felt for him rose to the surface. For the first time since her baby's death, she wanted to put her arms around her husband and be held in his. It was a fleeting connection but it served to galvanise her into action.

"I will try," she said to her mother. "I'll start a letter tonight. And perhaps in a few weeks time I'll look into booking a passage to Malaya; there's bound to be a delay before I can actually sail."

Theresa recounted to William the gist of her conversation with Gladys, adding:

"I wonder how long it will be before she travels to Malaya, when she can't even write to him yet?"

"Maybe she'll get like her mother was after the sister died - that took a couple of years, didn't it?"

"No, I don't think it will be that bad. It's probably a perfectly normal reaction. It must be terrible to lose a baby like that."

"She could at least write to him. He's out there, longing to hear from her, and if she hasn't even put pen to paper yet, it will be five or six weeks at least before he gets a letter."

"I suppose he'll just have to be patient. Henry has written to him, explaining, and you could write again and say how I found her - but y.ou'd better not say exactly what she said; she wouldn't want that to be passed on."

"I wouldn't tell him that anyway. He's hurting enough without hearing that his wife blames him for not being there."

"She wasn't blaming him, just saying that because of it he can't possibly feel as she does."

"Well, he's certainly feeling pretty bad. I haven't had such an unhappy letter from him since just after our mother died. The longer she delays writing and then travelling to Malaya, the worse it will be for their relationship; a rift will open up between them." Then he added: " He's spent nearly a decade of his life waiting for her, one way or another. Maybe it would have been better if he'd walked away from that cruise ship and never seen her again. I did warn him at the time that there could be pitfalls ahead, but of course he didn't listen!"

"Well, you could hardly have foreseen this event, even if you did anticipate Eliza's opposition. And they were so happy together last year. They are right for each other and I'm sure it will all work out in the end."

~ * ~

Meanwhile, in Malaya, Joss received Henry's first letter in the second week of April, and one from Will shortly after. The details of Gladys' illness and the birth and death of the baby made harrowing reading. He was glad that their daughter had been given a name but upset at the thought of her in an unmarked mass grave. Both Henry and Will emphasised that her soul had gone to heaven. 'To be with Alice' said Henry, and 'with our mother' according to Will. Joss viewed these statements with some degree of scepticism. The idea that Gladys' sister and his mother - who had never met in life - would somehow join forces to look after a newly arrived baby's soul, seemed far-fetched to him. He considered himself to be a Christian and believed in God and some form of afterlife, but had never subscribed to all the theology of the established church. He knew Gladys normally had her doubts too, but right now she would probably be finding it a comfort to think that their child was with her dead sister.

Alya's baby had been born in early April. It was a girl, whom they named Arianna Edith. On Joss' next visit, Theo ran out to him, bursting to impart the news that he had a little sister.

"Come and see her, Daddy. She can't play with me yet, but she will get bigger!"

Joss dutifully admired the baby and congratulated Alya and Jim. He noted that, unlike Theo, she was quite dark skinned. She seemed to be quite a placid baby who did not cry much. He wondered what characteristics their baby girl would have developed. He tried his best to be happy for Alya and Jim and to join in with Theo's enthusiasm, but it took considerable effort and he was quite glad to escape to the club for the evening.

By late April, he was eagerly scanning the mail for a letter from Gladys, but a further letter from Henry dashed his hopes.

"....does not feel able to write to you yet....recovering gradually physically but still very low in spirits..."

A letter from Will followed shortly afterwards, saying much the same thing, although merely reporting what he had heard from Henry. He added darkly that it was to be hoped that Gladys would not sink into a prolonged melancholic decline as her mother had done following the death of her sister. Already full of gloom after reading Henry's letter, Joss could have done without that comment. Henry's letter had been cautiously optimistic that Gladys would feel able to write in another week or two. Will had said that Theresa planned to visit her shortly. Joss hoped it would be soon, then he would have her first-hand account of how his wife was really faring. It was all so frustrating; the only method of communication they had was correspondence and each letter took five or six weeks to get between the countries. He longed to know what she was really feeling and thinking. By now she would have received his first letter and he had written twice since. In the weeks following the birth, letters had arrived from her which had been posted before she got ill. She had described how active the baby was becoming inside her and had gone into detail about the preparations for his or her arrival. It had all made very painful reading.

He wondered how long it would be before she was well enough to sail to join him. Probably it would now be several more months, perhaps not until the autumn. He reflected that they had now known and loved each other for nearly eight years, but had only spent a total of nine months together and only one month as a married couple. He put his head in his hands, despair threatening to take over, then mentally shook himself and reached for his writing pad. He wrote again, laying his soul bare, telling her how much he needed her and wanted to look after her, begging her to write soon and not delay sailing to join him.

"....we need to be together, to talk to each other, to let our love for one another start to heal the grief. Please, darling, don't shut me out....write and tell me how you are feeling and come to me as soon as you can.......you are precious to me beyond words..."

Her letter, which crossed with his, finally arrived at the beginning of June.

".....I'm sorry it's taken me so long to write. My heart and mind have been in a very dark place these last weeks. I was drowning in grief. I could think of nothing and no-one except our baby; my longing for her was so intense and all consuming that it blocked everything else from my thoughts........I still love you, my darling, but it seemed to me that you couldn't possibly be grieving as I was, not only because you are a man and did not carry her inside you for eight months nor give birth to her after hours of agonising labour, but also because you never even saw her or held her - all you did was supply the seed which made her. I felt that we would have no

point of connection...........I wasn't able to express my love for you because it was pushed right to the bottom of my heart, below Alicia.........I'm sorry if all this is hurtful to hear - it's not my intention to cause you pain - but I have to be honest......."

By the time he had finished reading, there were tears in his eyes. His need to be with her was intense; he desperately wanted to try to ease her pain, but he felt so far away from her in every sense. He also recognised that things would never be quite the same; they could not just take up where they had left off. The sorrow would always be with them and between them. However, her last paragraph, saying that she was going to look into available sailing dates to Malaya, had given him hope that it would not be too long before they were together and he could at least try to help her recover.

~ * ~

Despite her promise to Joss, Gladys continued to put off contacting the colonial office. She felt unequal to the task of organising everything, weary at the very thought of it all. It was the onset of warmer weather in May which spurred her into looking through her summer wardrobe and she realised that nothing fit properly; she had changed shape since the baby. She would also need more clothes suitable for a tropical climate; those she had bought in 1913 and hardly worn since were now dated. Despite her present apathy, she found herself starting to care again about what she wore. She did not want to cut a dowdy, old-fashioned figure in Kuala Lumpur society. She roused herself enough to visit her dressmaker and, having established how much time would be needed to alter some outfits and make new ones, she finally contacted the colonial office to book a passage, requesting late July or early August. Unfortunately, this was a busy period and she was offered the choice of late June - just a few weeks away - or 9th September.

Unable to face the thought of rushing all her preparations in order to make the June sailing, she accepted the September one and sent a letter to Joss advising him of her anticipated arrival date of 19th October in Singapore.

Having made that decision, she then had to get on with her preparations, but she took little pleasure in the process. Still crushed by grief, her former eagerness to start a new life in Malaya had gone. She did now want to be with Joss again and, had he arrived back in England, she would have fallen into his arms, but the thought of being in a strange new country, with people she did not know and unfamiliar customs, was now a daunting prospect, which she had to steel herself to face.

When she started to pack her trunk, Eliza asked whether she was going to take the baby clothes with her. "For your next baby?"

Gladys hesitated, then said firmly: "No. It would be tempting fate. If I am lucky enough to conceive again, then you can pack them up and send them to me."

By the end of August, with everything ready to go, she began to relax. Some of her fears had faded, along with much of her lethargy, and she began to tentatively look forward to being with Joss again.

~ * ~

When he received her letter, Joss breathed a sigh of relief. At last! For a week or two he was in a state of euphoria, day-dreaming about being with her again and allowing himself to blissfully anticipate their love-making. True to his resolve on their wedding day, he had been entirely faithful to her since his return to Malaya and could now hardly wait to revive their physical intimacy. Later, he started to think about more practical issues. Rural Raub, with its limited, male dominated social life was perhaps not the best place for Gladys to continue getting over the loss of their baby. There was also the near impossibility of continuing to visit Theo from here, once Gladys was living with him, and telling her about him was now totally out of the question. He put in a formal request for his next transfer to be back to Kuala Lumpur, giving his wife's arrival as the reason, explaining about the death of their baby and saying that he believed that she would be happier if she could immerse herself in the more extensive female social life in the capital. He received a reply to the effect that his personal circumstances would be taken into account in due course, but the possibility of a transfer before the end of the year was unlikely.

He started to prepare Theo for not seeing him for a few months from mid October. When he first broached the subject, Theo's face fell.

"Why not?"

"Because my wife is arriving from England, and she has been very poorly and also very sad and I will need to give her all my time and attention for a while; she will need a lot of looking after."

"Why is she sad?"

"Do you remember me telling you about the little baby who went to heaven?"

Theo nodded.

"Well, that was her baby girl, hers and mine, and she still misses her very much. "

Theo's not-quite-four-year-old mind tried to absorb this and make sense of the relationships.

"Is this baby my sister? Like Arianna? And the lady my auntie?"

"That's right. She was your little half-sister, and I suppose you could call Gladys your auntie, in the same way you call Jim Uncle."

"Why can't I meet Auntie Gladys?"

Joss took a deep breath. This conversation was getting out of hand.

"I hope you will be able to meet her one day, but not yet, I'm afraid. I'm really sorry, son. I'm going to miss you very much and I hope we won't be apart for too long. But I'll send you letters. Uncle

Jim can read them to you and, if you want to tell me things, you can ask him to write them down for you. And you can write your name at the bottom yourself now, can't you?" This was something Theo had just learned to do. "I hope to be transferred to Kuala Lumpur early next year and then I'll be able to visit you again, as it's only a short journey from there and I don't need to stay overnight."

To Theo, next year was an eternity away. Joss looked at his unhappy face, tears threatening to overflow, and felt he was being a cruel father, but what else could he do? He was caught in a trap of his own making. He hated having to choose between his wife and his son, and he thought sadly that this Christmas would be the first one spent apart from Theo. Last year, he had stayed two nights in Klang and had been able to watch him excitedly opening his stocking on Christmas day morning.

"Cheer up," he said now, giving the child a hug and wiping away his tears. "We've still got a couple of months left before then and I'll come here every other weekend. Let's make the most of our time together. What do you want to do now - shall we drive down to the port and see the ships?"

Joss had local leave due and he booked it to coincide with Gladys' arrival date. He would go to Singapore to meet her and accompany her up the coast on the local steamer. He wrote to his friend Hugh, a fellow 1903 cadet who was now assistant to the Chief Secretary of the FMS, asking if they could stay the first few days with him and his wife in Kuala Lumpur, then he reserved the following week in the Bukit Kutu hill station. He envisaged them having a second honeymoon.

~ * ~

Chapter 11

On Monday 8th September, Gladys set off by train to London, accompanied by Henry and Eliza. They were to stay overnight at Lavinia's house before heading to Tilbury the following morning. Over the weekend, she had said her farewells to the rest of her family, her friends and in-laws, and on each occasion, had felt a sinking in the pit of her stomach. As she had told them all, she would be back again sometime in 1922 as Joss was now entitled to take leave every four years, but this was presently scant comfort to her. Her fear of starting a new life in a strange and remote country had returned in full measure. She recalled Joss telling her that he too had been beset by last minute nerves all those years ago and, when it came to the final parting from his mother and brother, could hardly bear to tear himself away, but, once on the ship, all his fears had evaporated. She hoped that would be the case with her, but recognised the difference in perspective between a twenty-three year old man and a forty year old woman.

At the dock, she located her trunk, sent earlier, and arranged for its loading onto the ship, then noticed that embarkation had already commenced. Better not to prolong her farewells. She turned to her parents and hugged them both tightly. Eliza was crying and Henry's voice cracked as he bade her farewell. Before she disappeared into the ship, she turned and waved, part of her wanting to run back to them and go home.

As Joss had done with her, she went up on deck to see if her parents were still on the dock, but they had left by then. She turned to go back down to her cabin and came face to face with one of the women who had been with her on her last Malayan course in London.

"Gladys! It is, isn't it?"

"Yes! Caroline! How lovely to see you again! I'm sorry we lost touch."

"So am I. I suppose you're returning from leave, like me?"

"Actually, I'm heading out there for the first time."

Caroline's eyes widened. "What's been happening with you then, all these years?" She hooked her arm through Gladys'. "Come on, let's go and get a cup of tea and you can tell me all about it."

~ * ~

In mid September, Joss contracted a stomach bug which, unlike his previous experiences of these, did not clear up in twenty-four hours or so. He became increasingly ill as the days went by. The pain in his abdomen was intense, feeling as if knives were grinding away in his guts. He had a high fever and the diarrhoea was violent, frequent and urgent, often accompanied by vomiting. After noting his employer's escalating and increasingly hasty trips out to the thunderbox, Haziq thoughtfully provided him with a lidded bucket to be kept in his bedroom, for which he was very grateful, although somewhat embarrassed. Haziq brought him drinks at regular intervals and he knew he had to take in fluids as best he could, but even the thought of solid food was nauseating. He had sent a message to Arthur on the first day, saying he was unable to come in to the office, and Haziq followed this up with daily bulletins. On the fourth day, which was a Sunday, Arthur came to see him and found him in bed in a stuffy, stiflingly hot bedroom.

"For Christ's sake, Joss, you need some fresh air in here!" he exclaimed, throwing open a window. "I'll tell Haziq to leave it open during daylight hours, shall I?"

"Thanks. You'd better not come too near, Arthur. Don't want you catching whatever it is I've got."

"I expect it was something you ate. It will run its course eventually."

"I hope so. I don't want to still be ill when my wife arrives."

"That's not until mid October, isn't it? You've plenty of time to recover. I never heard of a tummy bug which went on that long."

"I think this must be dysentery."

"Even so, it should clear up in a couple of weeks. Don't rush back to the office though; give yourself time to convalesce. We're managing fine and I can always come and ask your advice if I need it."

After just over a week, his symptoms started to subside. Still very weak, he managed a few mouthfuls of food - which made him feel as full as if he had just eaten a three course meal - and then dragged himself to the bathroom for a much needed sluice down. While he was there, Haziq changed the bed linen. Later, he felt well enough to sit in a chair for a few hours and read a book, then he started writing a letter to his brother. There was no point in writing to Gladys as she had already set sail; Henry had sent him a telegram confirming they had seen her onto the ship. After a further day at home, by which time the diarrhoea seemed to have dried up completely, he ventured into the office for a few hours. Arthur had kept things going admirably, and he told him so.

"I'll get a good report then, will I, when they are ready to transfer me?!"

"You'll get a glowing one! Have you heard anything about a transfer?"

"They hinted at early December. I understand you've asked to go back to K.L. by the end of the year, and they want my successor to have a few weeks with you before you go."

As Joss had heard nothing further about his next post, this was welcome news - he and Gladys should be back in the capital in the New Year.

Two days later, after a Sunday spent taking it easy, he was in the office, intending to stay for a full day if he could, when the pain in his guts started up again. At first, it came and went and he told himself it was just trapped wind, then it became more constant and also more severe. It also felt different from before and was mainly concentrated in one area. He started to feel feverish again and nausea set in. After an hour or two of this, he told Arthur he was not feeling too good and would go home. As he stood up to leave, the pain became so intense that he gasped in agony and doubled up. Alarmed, Arthur asked:

"What's the matter - is it starting up again?"

"I don't know - maybe - but it feels different." Another spasm gripped him and this time he yelled out loud. "The pain was bad enough before, but it wasn't this unbearable!"

"I'd better drive you to the hospital," Arthur said firmly.

At the local hospital, being the District Officer, Joss received preferential treatment and was seen immediately. The young native doctor poked and prodded his belly, asking him where it hurt the most. When he had finished, he said:

"Your abdomen is very swollen and tender and, bearing in mind that you have just had a bout of dysentery, I think you probably have an ulcerated bowel, which may already have become perforated. You will need an operation without delay or peritonitis will set in. We can't do it here; you'll have to go to the European hospital at Kuala Lumpur. I'll tell your colleague to drive you there straight away."

Within a few minutes they were heading out of Raub and towards the mountains. Arthur had suggested that Joss might be more comfortable lying across the back seat. The pain came and went and at its most intense, he sometimes passed out for a few minutes. Twice, he had to ask Arthur to stop the car so that he could vomit into the bushes. After what seemed an eternity to Joss, they arrived at the hospital, where he was seen as an emergency, and given a thorough examination. The English doctor confirmed the diagnosis and the need for an operation.

"We'll carry it out first thing in the morning. You must not eat or drink anything before then and I'll prescribe something to ease the pain a little."

He was allocated a bed in a side ward and given a hospital gown to wear. Arthur came with him to the ward.

"I'll have to stay the night here," he said. " I can beg a bed in the cadets' mess. I'll need to contact the authorities and let them know about you. Then I'll come to see you in the morning before I go back. Is there anyone else you'd like me to contact?"

"Yes, please. Would you get hold of my friend Hugh - he's the Chief Sec.'s assistant. Please ask him to come to see me before I have this operation; there's something I need to ask him to do. He'll also be able to deal with the red tape for you; you shouldn't need to go to the government offices as well. He may even put you up for the night. Oh, and would you please telephone Jim, the D.O. at Klang, and let him know. I was supposed to be visiting Theo this coming weekend. There's a telephone line to Klang from here now. And thanks, Arthur, for everything - you're a good chap, one of the best!"

Hugh arrived later that evening. Joss was dosing by then, but heard his Scottish accent, speaking to the nurse outside the door.

"He's asked to see me urgently, before you operate on him. He won't mind if he's woken up!"

Sitting on the edge of the bed, Hugh surveyed his friend. "Gosh, you look peaky, old chap!"

"Has Arthur found somewhere for the night?"

"Yes, I told him he can stay at our place and he's heading over there now. We've phoned Klang, by the way, and Jim sends you his best wishes. He'll explain to Theo."

"I hope I'm not laid up for too long. I need to be well enough to meet Gladys off the ship."

Hugh looked doubtful. "That might be pushing it a bit. It will probably take you several weeks to recover; you may even still be in hospital then. But don't worry - I'll arrange for your wife to be met and I'll bring her here myself if I can."

"This is the last thing she needs, me being an invalid, after all she's gone through. I need to look after her, not the other way round."

"Well, it's out of your hands, isn't it? And it might even be good for her to have to look after you for a bit - take her mind off her loss."

Changing the subject, Joss said: "Hugh, can I ask you to do something for me, should I not make it through this operation?"

"Don't say that! Of course you'll come through it."

"There's no guarantee. You know that. People often do die after or during operations. If the worst does happen, my things will be packed up and given to Gladys. Before that's done, can you get my houseboy to retrieve a small package from the top dresser drawer in my bedroom, which is addressed to my brother, and see that it gets to him, without Gladys seeing it? And there's also a letter addressed to Alya, to be taken or sent to her. Both items concern Theo."

"Yes, I'll take care of all that, *if* it becomes necessary. Don't worry."

"And please tell Gladys how very much I love her, and that I would want her to find happiness with someone else later on, if she can. She must not mourn me forever."

"Yes, I'll tell her - if I have to!"

"She must never find out about Theo, not after losing our baby. It would cause her too much heartache."

"She won't hear it from me, and Elizabeth doesn't know, so she can't let it slip. Now, stop worrying about everything, and just concentrate on getting better. I'll come and see you tomorrow, after you're out of the operating theatre."

135

"There's just one more thing: I would have given Arthur a first class report at the end of his time in Raub. Would you tell them that, please? I don't want him to miss out."

"I expect you'll be able to do the report yourself, but if you can't, I'll pass that on. Now, get some sleep - and good luck for tomorrow!"

Sleep did not come easily to Joss. Apart from the pain, which was only dulled by the medication, he was feeling very scared. Surgery was known to be an extremely risky enterprise. 'I'm not ready to die yet,' he thought. Probably no-one ever was, but perhaps it was easier to reconcile to after a long life, when you were starting to feel old and weary. His married life had scarcely begun; they had all that ahead of them still. How devastating it would be for Gladys if she arrived to find him dead, on top of the loss of their baby. And Theo, who was not yet four years old. He would retain only vague memories of him, as Will had of their father. Jim would become his father, but at least he would be a good one.

The next morning, Hugh and Arthur arrived at the hospital just as Joss was being wheeled back to the ward. He was still unconscious. Hugh sought out the doctor who had carried out the procedure.

"It's going to be touch and go, I'm afraid. Peritonitis had already set in quite extensively. We've done what we can; what happens now is in God's hands."

Arthur returned to Raub, Hugh having promised to keep him informed. Hugh waited until Joss came round from the anaesthetic, but when he did, he was still groggy and drowsy and not making much sense.

An official telegram was sent to William Henry Goldthorp in Heckmondwike, England, advising him that his brother was seriously ill in hospital. Nothing could be done about informing Mrs Gladys Goldthorp until her ship docked in Colombo. It was hoped that there would be better news by then.

It took three days for Joss to die. For much of that time he was delirious, with only a few brief lucid spells. Periodically, he addressed the fair-haired doctor attending him as Will and the dark-haired nurse as Gladys. Hugh came in each day after work and once or twice Joss seemed to recognise him. At times, his mind drifted back to his earlier life and fragmented images floated into his vision: his first day at school, at barely four years old......larking around with Will and other children in the streets near their home.....Will trying to warm his feet on him in winter in the bed they had shared......the sound of his mother's sewing machine.......the library and quad at his grammar school.......rowing on the river at Oxford on a bright summer's day..... his first sight of Penang Harbour ...... the heady days of his blossoming romance with Gladys.

As the poison circulated in his blood stream, and his vital organs shut down one by one, he sank into a deep coma. The medical staff sent an urgent message to Hugh to let him know that there was very little time left. As the end neared, Joss dreamed he was travelling through a long narrow tunnel, towards an extremely bright light. As he drew closer, he saw the figure of his mother silhouetted in the light and beside her was a man who looked rather like Will, but somehow he knew it was not his brother. As he reached them, a profound sense of peace spread through him.

"Time of death 12.03 pm," the doctor intoned.

Hugh released Joss' hand, which he had been holding for the past half-hour, and looked sadly down at his friend. Sixteen years ago, four of them had set sail together for the East, young men eager to start their new life in Malaya, and now two of the four were dead.

'This cursed country,' he thought. 'They would both be still alive, had they stayed in England.'

The nurse's voice broke into his thoughts. "He seems to have died peacefully. Look, there's even a slight smile on his face."

"So there is. I shall tell his wife and brother that; it may be of some comfort to them."

Joss was buried the following day, in the Venning Road protestant cemetery. The funeral was of a military character, as befitted a senior government official who was also a corporal in the Malay Volunteer Rifles. Men wearing that uniform carried the coffin. It was well-attended, despite the short notice. The Chief Secretary was there, along with the Residents of Pahang and Selangor, and the acting High Commissioner had sent a representative. Many of Joss' friends and colleagues, from throughout the FMS and Straits Settlements, managed to make it in time, including Jim from Klang, Arthur from Raub and Hugh and his wife, Elizabeth. Many others sent wreaths and the grave was covered with flowers.

"They gave him a good send-off," Jim said to Hugh afterwards.

"Indeed. What have you said to his small son? Have you told him?"

"We've tried. I'm not sure he completely understands. I think he thinks that people just visit heaven and then come back, and perhaps it's best if he continues to believe that for now."

~ * ~

Chapter 12

On the ship, after having been very seasick as they sailed across the Bay of Biscay, Gladys had by now found her sea legs and was enjoying the voyage. The first-class passengers led a fairly luxurious life on board; there was fine dining, and dancing and entertainment in the evenings. She and Caroline had resurrected their friendship. Caroline was travelling with her husband and two small children, a boy of four and a girl of two. Her husband, John, said that he knew Joss very slightly.

"You met him too, once or twice, I think," he said to his wife. "At the Selangor club, during the later years of the war. Fair-haired chap, mid thirties, Yorkshire accent."

"I vaguely recall him. I mustn't have registered his first name or I would have connected him with Gladys - she was always talking about him!"

Later, in their cabin, John mentioned to his wife something else about Joss:

"It was rumoured that he had an Asian mistress and a child by her. He used to visit them weekends, or so it was said."

"Well, for God's sake don't let that slip in front of Gladys! I'm pretty sure she has no idea. And it must be over now."

"With the mistress, maybe, but what about the child?"

John and Caroline had been living in Singapore before their leave and were due to return there.

"You and Joss must come to visit us," Caroline said to Gladys.

As the voyage progressed, bringing her ever closer to the love of her life, Gladys found her desire for physical intimacy with him returning in full force. At night she lay in her bunk aching to feel his body pressed against hers, longing for his touch. She had been starved of his love for too long and wanted once again to be as close as two people could be with each other. She fantasised about their reunion and imagined them recreating the heady, love-drenched days of their honeymoon. She hoped he would not mind her stretch marks and her slightly changed shape, and she anxiously surveyed herself in the mirror for signs of aging. Although her face had matured, she luckily had the kind of bone structure which retains beauty well into middle age and beyond. Furthermore, the sea air had agreed with her and had had a rather rejuvenating effect, she decided. She looked better than she had for a long time.

When the ship docked at Colombo, she went ashore with Caroline and John for a few hours. She drank in the sights and sounds of the East and was thrilled by them, despite the suffocating heat and humidity. 'I'll get used to that,' she thought.

When they returned to the ship, there was a telegram awaiting her. She looked at it for a moment or two before opening it, puzzled and slightly apprehensive.

.....*Very sorry to inform you. After a short illness and an operation Joss Wood Goldthorp died Friday 3rd October. Buried the following day in the Venning Road cemetery in Kuala Lumpur. Condolences for your loss. You will be met at Singapore by a government official.*

Although she read the words and took in their individual meanings, her mind refused to absorb the reality of the situation they conveyed. She had a sense of time standing still and she felt unreal, apart from the world around her, as though there were an invisible curtain between her and other people. At the same time, she felt as if she were outside herself, looking at herself from afar.

Seeing her white, shocked face, Caroline asked her what had happened, and, receiving no reply, gently took the telegram from her and read it.

"Oh, my God!" she exclaimed. "Oh, Gladys, my dear, what can I say? How awful! You must be devastated."

John took the telegram from her. He found himself at a loss what to say or do.

"You must come and stay with us," Caroline said, "until you return to England."

"She'll be going to Kuala Lumpur first," John said, "they'll take her there."

"Then afterwards. You need to be with friends."

To Gladys, her voice seemed to be coming from far away and she heard her as if in a dream. Why was she talking about returning to England? She left them without speaking and returned to her cabin. Her mind totally rejected the words she had read; it was as if they did not apply to her, to Joss. She continued to focus on their reunion, but at the same time she felt cold and numb, as if all capacity to feel had drained out of her. She stayed in that state of mind for the remainder of the voyage.

"I can't get through to her," Caroline said to John. "She's just not accepting it at all; still talking about being with him again - on the few occasions when she says anything at all. It's as though she never read that telegram. Do you think she thinks it's a mistake?"

"I don't know. I've heard of people's minds shutting down, rejecting reality. I suppose that's what she's doing. She's in a state of shock, but it will hit her eventually."

~ * ~

Meanwhile, in Heckmondwike, William read the Malayan Government's first telegram with mounting trepidation. He showed it to Theresa.

"What do you think 'abdominal operation' means exactly?" she asked.

He shrugged. "No idea. What kinds of abdominal operations are there?"

"Appendicitis?"

141

"Could be."

"He hasn't already had that out?"

"No. He's never had anything out! And he's always been in robust health."

"Well, that will stand him in good stead, won't it, with his recovery."

"Let's hope so. But it says he's seriously ill, and it was sent after the operation."

"Probably immediately after. He could already be getting better. Did he mention any health problems in his last letters?"

"No, but I suppose there could be one still in the post."

William continued to worry over the next several days, during which they heard nothing further. He said an extra prayer each night for his brother's speedy recovery. He hardly dared to dwell on the worst case scenario. Joss had always been a hugely important person in his life; he could scarcely envisage a world without him in it. One of his earliest memories was of his baby brother toddling towards him on uncertain legs, holding out his hand for some toy. In those early days, Will had sometimes found him rather annoying, but as they grew older and Joss left babyhood behind, the relatively small age difference between them had gradually ceased to matter and they had become each other's best friend. They had had their disagreements, and occasional fights, but had never fallen out for long. During the many adult years they had spent far apart, they had always kept in regular contact by letter. He tried to push the niggling thought that Joss might die to the back of his mind, but was unable to banish it completely and it made him tense, inclined to be sharp with his staff at the shop and short-fused with his younger children, whose often boisterous behaviour jarred with his present mood.

The second telegram arrived as the family were having their tea. Nerves fluttering in his stomach, Will slit the envelope open. He read the brutal words, advising of Joss' death and burial, and the

142

colour drained from his face. He pushed back his chair and abruptly left the room. Theresa picked up the telegram and read it quickly.

"Oh, no!" she exclaimed.

Donald reached across his sister and took the telegram from his mother. He and Mabel read it together. Her eyes filled with tears.

"Oh poor Uncle Joss! And poor Auntie Gladys - she's still on her way there, isn't she? And he's already been buried!"

Leslie reached across the table and picked up the telegram. He and Ewart read it and looked sadly at each other, neither of them knowing what to say. No-one enlightened Stanley, not yet able to read, who looked from one to the other of them in bewilderment.

Theresa pushed back her chair and stood up. "Take charge of things down here, please, Donald. I need to go to your father."

"Do you remember that day in Blackpool?" Donald asked his sister, as their mother left the room.

She nodded sadly.

"We had such fun, didn't we? He was always fun to be with."

Theresa climbed the stairs and found Will in their bedroom, sitting on the edge of the bed. He was staring unseeingly out of the window, tears slowly coursing down his face, steeped in memories of a shared childhood. She wrapped her arms around him and he laid his head on her shoulder. They sat on like that, neither moving nor speaking, through the gathering dusk, until the darkness completely enveloped them.

~ * ~

As they prepared for landing at Singapore, Gladys was half expecting to see Joss there, waiting for her as he had promised. At the same time, she knew he would not be. On one level, she was fully aware of what had happened, but was still unable to absorb it emotionally. She felt imprisoned in a cold hard shell which prevented her from feeling or reacting to anything, or relating to other people. As they disembarked, she automatically scanned the waiting crowds for Joss but was not surprised at being unable to see him. Then they saw a young man carrying a placard with her name on it in large letters. John escorted her over to him.

"Mrs Goldthorp? I'm David Feldman. I've been sent to accompany you up the coast to Port Klang and then on to Kuala Lumpur. Please accept my sincere condolences for your terrible loss."

Gladys looked at him blankly for a moment, then found her voice and her manners. She greeted him and thanked him, but in a flat, expressionless tone. David explained that Hugh had been unable to come to Singapore himself, but would meet them at Kuala Lumpur rail station. She would be staying with him and his wife. Gladys nodded; Joss had written that they were to stay a few days with Hugh and Elizabeth.

The voyage up the coast on the local steamer seemed interminable to both of them. The only way Gladys could cope, and stay safely within her shell, was to imagine that Joss was waiting for her at Hugh's house - or perhaps was still in hospital, not yet recovered enough from his illness to be discharged. She knew, deep down, that this was a fantasy, but she needed it to sustain her; the reality was still too appalling to be faced. For his part, David, a cadet in his early twenties, had not relished this assignment of escorting a newly widowed woman and was now unsure whether it was turning out better or worse than he had expected. He had anticipated weeping, an excess of emotion, and had steeled himself to deal with that. He now found himself not knowing what to say to this quiet, expressionless woman who initiated no conversation and responded to his comments about the coastal scenery with the barest minimum of words.

At Kuala Lumpur station the following morning, Hugh grasped Gladys' hand in both of his large ones and told her how dreadfully sorry he was for her loss.

"I was with him at the end. I can assure you that it was very peaceful."

These words, uttered in a comforting Scottish burr, threatened to penetrate Gladys' armour and she was unable to respond with more than a nod of acknowledgement. As they waited for her trunk to be loaded into the car, David found the opportunity to take Hugh aside.

"She's hardly spoken a dozen words to me all the way here, and she doesn't seem to react to anything much."

Hugh nodded. "Grief takes people in different ways. Joss described her as outgoing, so she's obviously not her usual self. I suppose it hasn't really hit her yet. We'll have to be ready to deal with an explosion of grief once it finally does!"

David handed him a piece of paper. "The people she was with on the ship gave me this, to pass on to you. It's their address in Singapore. They want her to stay with them before she returns to England and have also asked that we keep them informed about how she is. They seemed very worried about her."

At Hugh's spacious, elegant residence, Gladys was introduced to Elizabeth, a pretty blonde in her early thirties, and their four year old daughter, Irene. Elizabeth was not a Scot and had an upper-class English accent. She grasped both Gladys' hands in hers and warmly expressed her sympathy.

"The maid will show you to your room and help you unpack. I hope you have all you need. Come through when you are ready; there will be refreshments waiting."

Before returning to his office, Hugh told his wife what David had said.

"We'd better show her the grave as soon as possible then," she responded. "I'll take her this afternoon."

They took a rickshaw to the cemetery in Venning Road. This was a novel experience for Gladys, which she would normally have relished, but she made no comment on their mode of transport.

"Hugh and some of Joss' other friends are arranging for a memorial cross to go on his grave," Elizabeth explained, as they approached the gate. "It will probably be erected in a couple of weeks time and hopefully you'll be able to see it before you leave."

As they entered the cemetery and she saw all the white headstones stretching ahead into the distance, cracks started to appear in Gladys' shell and a sensation of cold, sickening dread settled in the pit of her stomach.

"It's just over there," Elizabeth said, pointing to a new plot which still contained the dead and dying remains of floral wreaths. Gladys halted in her tracks.

"Would you mind leaving me here for a while? I think I'd rather do this on my own." Her voice sounded less flat than before and Elizabeth detected suppressed emotion.

"Of course, if that's what you want. But are you sure you'll be alright?"

She nodded.

"I'll come back for you in half an hour or so. You don't know your way around the city yet, so wait for me here, won't you?"

"Yes, I will. Thank you."

Elizabeth turned and headed for the exit. She was somewhat anxious about leaving her charge, but, on the other hand, rather glad to be spared the outpouring of grief which must surely be coming.

As Gladys came up to the grave and read the inscription on the headstone, the icy numbness, which had had her in its grip since Colombo, finally melted away and the full force of her loss slammed into her. Grief tore through her as a bolt of physical agony and she gasped with the intensity of it. She screamed out his name, over and over, then sank to her knees in front of the freshly dug earth, laid her head against the cold hard headstone and wept. Great gulping sobs shook her slight frame. She wept for the loss of the sight, sound, smell and touch of the man she loved so much, for the end of her hopes and dreams, for their dead baby and for all the wasted years

146

spent apart. She cried until she had no tears left, until she was drained of all emotion, then she curled up in a foetal position on top of the grave - which was how Elizabeth found her on her return.

~ * ~

When Hugh had taken delivery of Joss' two letters, retrieved from the bungalow in Raub, he had despatched the one for Alya straight away, but put the one addressed to William aside until he had time to write a covering letter, describing Joss' final days and his funeral. It was not until shortly before Christmas that his letter arrived in Heckmondwike. It came in the second post, after Will had left for the shop, and Theresa propped it up on the mantelpiece. She knew it was not another letter from Joss, written before he got ill - like one they had already received - as the handwriting was not his. When Will arrived home, she drew his attention to it. He fingered it, then put it back down.

"I'll open it later, after the children are all in bed. It's probably just an official letter with belated condolences."

Donald took longer than usual finishing his homework, so Will took the letter into the front room where he could read it in peace, bidding his eldest son goodnight, so he would not be disturbed. By now, some of the raw edges of his grief had worn a little smoother, but Joss' handwriting on the enclosed thick, inner envelope, addressed to him with the words ' In the event of my death' still gave him a jolt. He read Hugh's covering letter first. He opened with an apology for the delay in sending on the enclosure, explained who he was and then told Will that Gladys had become very ill after visiting Joss' grave and had been hospitalised for a while.

.....her life was despaired of at one point and the doctors were at a loss as to whether she had picked up some illness on the journey or whether her symptoms were caused by grief, or a combination of the two. However, she is now recovering and will be discharged in a

147

day or two, to convalesce with us. After that, she plans to visit some friends in Singapore whom I believe she met on the ship.......

Will was already aware of most of this, from Gladys' family, who had been sent telegrams. The letter continued with an account of Joss' last days, his funeral, and a synopsis of the events leading up to his admission to hospital, as recounted to Hugh by Arthur.

.....I was with him for a part of each day while he was in hospital and I was there at the end. I held his hand as he departed this world. It was very peaceful and he died with a smile on his face. During those final days, he would partly recover consciousness periodically and he spoke your name several times, as well as Gladys'. ....The night before his operation he asked me to retrieve the enclosed from his house and send it to you, should the worst happen. He did not want Gladys to find it and perhaps open it by mistake, and when you have seen the contents you will understand why.......

Will blinked hard and wiped his hand over his eyes, then put Hugh's letter aside and opened the enclosure. There was a long letter in his brother's handwriting, a folded document and another envelope containing photographs. He read the letter first, which was dated December 1918.

.....If you are reading this, it is because I am no longer alive. I can hazard a guess as to how you might be feeling about that, as I know how I would feel if I lost you, but try not to grieve for me too much. After all, if your firmly held beliefs are correct - and I hope they are - I will have gone to a better place, where I will be with our parents and one day you will join us........ ..You will not be pleased with what I am about to tell you - if I were still alive you would berate me soundly, as I deserve........I make no excuses for my actions, but, at the start of the war, after our wedding had been cancelled, I was at a very low ebb. I had no idea when the war would end, when Gladys and I would be together - even if we ever would be. Try to understand what I did in that context.........the

148

relationship only lasted a year; I could not take her with me to the capital, but by then she was expecting our son.

At this point, Will drew in a sharp breath and paused in his reading for a moment.

..... I don't need to tell you how it feels to hold your baby for the first time. I was overwhelmed with love for him..........he's a lovely, sunny natured little boy, just turned three as I am writing this. Although he's a Eurasian, he could easily pass for a British child - as you can see for yourself from the photographs - and he's growing up bilingual.............I wanted so much to tell you about him when I was in England; I nearly blurted it out on a couple of occasions (and you suspected I was holding something back). I was so afraid that either you or Theresa would consider it your duty to tell Gladys and she would call off the wedding. I was also uncertain how you would react; I envisaged you perhaps disowning me and banishing me from your home and your family...............I don't know what age Theo will have reached by the time you are reading this, but I hope that you can find it in your heart to acknowledge him as your nephew and your children's cousin..............His stepfather, Jim, will be retiring and returning to England with his family in about ten years time and Theo will come with them. That would be an opportunity for him to meet his paternal relatives. He and Stanley are the same age - perhaps they could write to each other in the meantime, once they are a few years older?............Of course, it is up to you to decide. I don't want to put pressure on you from beyond the grave. You may hate the very idea of a mixed race, illegitimate nephew and want nothing to do with him, but I hope you can forgive me for what I did and not visit the sins of the father upon the child...........Please, do not think too badly of me and do not let this sully your memories...........Alya and Jim's address is the same one I had when I was in Klang, i.e...................I hope you will decide to contact them.............Please say goodbye from me to Theresa, Mabel and the boys. All my love, as always, Joss.............P.S. One final request:

Gladys must never find out about Theo, for her sake. She has been through enough.

As Will put the letter down, his mind in turmoil, Theresa came into the room. She sat down next to him and looked at him questioningly. He handed her Hugh's letter, with Joss' below it, then he unfolded the document, already guessing what it was.

Certified copy of an entry of birth......2nd November 1915.....Klang, Pahang.....Theodore William...boy....father Joss Wood Goldthorp.......

He opened the small packet of photographs and found himself looking into his brother's eyes. The resemblance was uncanny - he could have been looking at Joss at the same age. He rifled through them; they were marked on the back with the ages, from two months to three years, with several taken at two years old. He would be four now, like Stanley.

Theresa finished reading the two letters. She was shocked by her brother-in-law's revelation.

"How do you feel about this?" she asked her husband. "Are you going to contact them, acknowledge the child?"

"I think so, yes. He's my nephew, my flesh and blood, and he looks so like Joss - look!"

He passed her the photographs, then got up and went to the bureau drawer where his own were kept. He found one of Joss at about three years old and put it side by side with Theo's.

"My goodness, yes, they are alike!" Theresa exclaimed.

"I can't reject him. I'm going to write to the stepfather as Joss asked. I hope you can support me in this?"

She nodded. "If that's what you want. I can understand it. Shall we tell the children?"

"Perhaps not yet. Let's wait and see how this fellow Jim responds. Meanwhile, we must keep this quiet from the Healeys."

~ * ~

In September 1923, Gladys returned to Joss' grave for a final visit before she sailed back to England. For the last four years, she had made a life for herself in Singapore. Her widow's pension from the Colonial Service, supplemented by the income from a part-time job in a school, had enabled her to live well, and, with John and Caroline's help, she had developed a good social life, although nothing could fill the gaping void in her soul. However, her mother's health was now failing and both Henry and Frank had entreated her to return home. Although she still fostered some residual resentment against Eliza for keeping her and Joss apart before the war, she also remembered her mother's devoted nursing when she had the Spanish flu and her support after the baby's death, and knew she could not desert her in her hour of need.

As she approached the grave, carrying flowers, she saw that someone else was there; an Asian woman with a small boy, about seven or eight years old, who looked European. The woman was engaged in arranging flowers in the stone vase. Assuming she must be an *ayah* (nanny) with her charge, Gladys wondered what their connection was to Joss. As she came up to them, the child turned to face her and she felt a frisson of shock - was it her imagination, or did this boy look very like Joss? Any doubt was quickly dispelled when he spoke.

"Have you come to say hello to my Daddy too?"

Shock rendered her temporarily speechless.

The woman spoke. "Are you one of Joss' friends? We will go in a minute and leave you in peace."

Gladys found her voice. "No, please don't go yet! I need to know who you are and why this boy is referring to my husband as 'Daddy'!"

There was a brief silence. "I'm so very sorry," Alya said. "You must be Gladys. I had no idea you were still in the country - I thought you'd returned to England years ago."

"Who is this child? Is he Joss' son?"

"Yes."

Gladys sat down heavily on the edge of the grave, feeling suddenly faint. "Please tell me," she said shakily, swallowing the bile which had risen up in her throat, "how this came about. Who is his mother?"

"I am."

"You?! You slept with my husband?!" Sudden fury swept over her.

"He wasn't your husband then, although you were promised to each other. I lived with Joss during the first year of the war, after your wedding had been cancelled."

"You lived with him! When he was engaged to me!"

"Yes, but if it's any consolation, Joss never loved me. His heart always belonged to you. But he did love Theo - very much - and he continued to see him regularly."

The boy was watching them, absorbing all of this.

"Are you Auntie Gladys?" he asked.

"My name's Gladys, yes."

Alya explained that he called his stepfather 'Uncle' and when Joss had told him about his wife in England, he had assumed she would be his auntie.

"You speak English well," Gladys said.

"Joss taught me initially and my husband is English. Theo is bilingual. He goes to an English school and he's doing well. He's a very clever boy."

"Like his father."

"Yes."

Theo interjected. "Daddy's in heaven now, isn't he? With your baby."

Had Joss told him about that? While she was half out of her mind with grief, was he telling his other child all about their baby?

152

"Joss grieved terribly for your little girl," Alya said, "and he had to explain to Theo why he was so sad." Then she added: "I know this must be a terrible shock to you, but don't think too badly of him. He always felt very guilty about betraying you, but men have needs and no-one knew how long the war would last."

Gladys found that she felt less betrayed by Joss' infidelity with this woman than by his deceit in never telling her he had a son. All those months in England, when she had thought they were so close, he had been keeping his sordid secret. When their baby had died, he had written telling her how devastated he was, all the time seeking solace with the child he already had. It hurt terribly.

As if guessing her thoughts, Alya said: "He wanted to tell you about Theo; he hated keeping it from you, but he was afraid that you'd call off the wedding. He intended to tell you after you had arrived in Malaya and settled in, but then you lost the baby and he felt that he couldn't cause you any more pain."

"Did his brother in England know about Theo?" Gladys asked.

Alya shook her head. "No, but Joss left a letter for him which was sent on after he died, so he knows now. He wrote to my husband and he sends Theo Christmas and birthday cards. He suggested that Theo could write to his cousins in England if he wants to, but so far he hasn't shown any interest in doing that. He has many cousins here, in my family, and two younger half-sisters."

Alya finished arranging the flowers she had brought. "There's room for yours as well - shall I arrange them for you?"

Wordlessly, Gladys handed them over. Her mind was in turmoil. Theo was watching her and she looked up and met his eyes, Joss' eyes. Suddenly, somewhere deep in her heart, she was glad that a part of Joss lived on in this child.

Alya said goodbye and turned to leave. Theo made to follow her.

"Goodbye, Auntie Gladys."

"Goodbye. I'm glad to have met you, Theo - you are so very like your father." She realised that she really meant it.

She stayed by the grave for a while longer, thoughts swirling around in her head. She needed to readjust her memories of Joss; he had fallen off the pedestal she had always placed him on and proved to be flawed. Despite that, her love for him and her grief at his loss were in no way lessened. Had he lived to tell her about Theo, she believed that she would have forgiven him - eventually.

End of Part III

Epilogue

May 1935 - Yorkshire

William, Theresa and Mabel, dressed in their best dark-coloured outfits, were setting off from their home in Milton Street, Heckmondwike, to attend a funeral. Donald and his wife Jennie were to join them at the crematorium. Stanley was minding the shop in their absence; William's oldest and youngest sons had followed him into the business. Leslie and Ewart had both become teachers and Ewart now lived in Bristol.

After the service - which was brief and simple in accordance with Gladys' written wishes - they lingered to talk to Frank.

"She's with him again, at last," he said reflectively. "She never got over his death. She had a couple of offers of marriage over the years, from widowers, but turned them down. She couldn't contemplate a life with anyone else. She could never settle in England again either, as you know. After Father died, the ownership of the house passed to her, but she was still off as soon as she could make the arrangements. India, America.......the doctors believe that she picked up her illness in India; Banti's disease is quite rare in Europe, but common there. She only returned home when her health was failing - basically she came home to die."

Then he changed the subject. "Did you ever hear from Joss' son?"

William was taken aback. "She told you about that, then? When she came to see us, after her initial return to England, she seemed quite adamant that she would not tell her family and asked us not to mention it if we saw any of you."

Frank nodded. "She never told our parents. But after Father died, she told me. I must say, I was not impressed with your brother's behaviour!"

"Neither was I, I can assure you, and If he'd spoken to me about it while he was still alive, I'd have told him so - in no uncertain terms!"

"She forgave him, though. Although, if they are together now in the afterlife, I bet she's giving him merry hell!"

They all laughed, and the mood somewhat lightened.

"To answer your original question," Will said, "no, I never heard from Theo. I had a nice letter back from his stepfather, and he said he'd encourage him to write to us when he was older, but there's been nothing since. He'll be nineteen now and they'll have been in England for some years, but I have no idea where. It's a shame; I would have liked to have met my nephew."

1982 - Kuala Lumpur

At the protestant cemetery in Venning Road, labourers were engaged in dismantling graves, as the site was to be redeveloped. Headstones were being lifted up, broken apart and thrown onto skips.

A young English student, working his way round the world on a gap year, was one of the temporary workers.

"What will happen to the bodies?" he asked the foreman, who spoke fairly good English.

"They will all be exhumed and then they'll be reburied in a large plot at the back of the main cemetery in Cheras Road."

"What?! All together, in one mass grave?"

"Yes."

"But there'll be a memorial plaque, listing who they all are?"

156

"Not as far as I know. The plans just show a basic metal sign indicating that the plot contains the remains relocated from Venning Road. No-one's been given the job of listing the details on the headstones."

"But have their relatives been consulted?"

"Shouldn't think so - they're mostly British anyway, from before Independence, and many of them were buried in the previous century. None of them will have relatives here."

Jason looked at the imposing memorial cross he was about to prise up from its moorings.

"This one has this large, ornate memorial. There were people who cared enough to have it erected and they would have expected it to last. Look, he didn't die until 1919 and he was only 39; he may well have younger relatives in England who would remember him - surely they should be told?"

The foreman shrugged. "Not our concern. How would the authorities know who they are, anyway?"

"Did anyone ever try to find out?"

"Don't expect so. Now you'd better get on and demolish that cross, if you want to be paid at the end of the day!"

The End

Author's Note

When I started to research my paternal family history, all I knew about Joss was that my father had had an uncle who had gone to Oxford University and then lived in Malaya. I had a vague recollection from 1972 - when I had been about to head off on a lengthy back-packing trip to that part of the world - of him asking me to make enquiries in Kuala Lumpur as to what had happened to his uncle. I must have misremembered that, as he would have known about his death, being ten years old at the time, and he had probably just asked me to find the grave. In the event, that trip did not extend to Malaysia, but my defective memory forty-odd years later caused me to waste some time looking for Joss and Gladys' deaths in the Japanese camps during World War II.

When I eventually turned up the final tragedy of their relationship, I knew it was a story crying out to be told. Originally, I planned it to be just a longish short story, but the characters and my imagination took over and it has become a book.

All the Goldthorps and Mallinsons featured, and all the Healeys, except Aunt Lavinia, are real people whose lives are documented in birth, marriage and death certificates, wills, census returns, passenger lists and newspaper archives. All these sources have produced a wealth of information which has provided the basic structure of the story and some of the detail. The rest is my imagination. I have neither deviated from nor omitted any of the true facts I uncovered - even when they were slightly inconvenient for the flow of the story and required me to research such matters as the marriage laws of the period and journey times in Colonial Malaya. I have used their real names, as all the people concerned are now dead, but I have left out the actual numbers of the houses they lived in, only naming the streets, in case the present owners may object.

The remaining characters are wholly fictitious, except for Theresa's cleaning lady, Hugh and Ernie, who are based on real people.

The Goldthorps were half of my family, therefore known to me in their later lives. I have scant memory of William, who died when I was five and had been ill for some time prior to that, but I remember Theresa as an old lady and I knew all their children as adults. My father was Leslie. I have brought in a few early indications of their characters and tastes; Ewart loved dogs and cars and Leslie became an accomplished musician. In her later years, Mabel talked a bit about Joss to one of my cousins and she seemed to have quite fond memories of him.

It was documented in a Malay newspaper article that Joss and Gladys met in 1911 (on a cruise in Scotland as described) but the genealogical evidence makes it clear that they remained in different countries between October 1911 and February 1918 and again from shortly after their marriage. The war only accounts for part of those periods. My explanations for those separations are pure invention, but I believe that they are feasible. Gladys' sister did die in the circumstances described and, although no living child was born to Joss and Gladys, stillbirths were not registered in those days.

I have endeavoured to keep the historical background and detail accurate, both in England and Malaya, and to avoid any modern day idioms creeping into speech.

People's characters and behaviour are partly shaped by the times and societies they live in. I have no idea what Joss was really like, but his nephews were all fundamentally decent men, so I have portrayed him as a basically nice person, with a conscience, but also a product of both his original humble background and the much more upper class circles in which he moved from the age of eighteen.

Religion played a much greater part in people's lives then than it does now and moral codes were far more rigid. However, sexual morality in colonial Malaya was more lax than that prevailing in England at the time, largely owing to the delayed marriages of men serving in the colonies and the uneven ratio of men to women. Asian mistresses were by no means uncommon, and although Alya and Theo are a product of my imagination, it is not outside the bounds of possibility that my cousins and I have some distant relatives in Malaysia!

With reference to the final part of the epilogue, I brought the issue of the relocated graves to the attention of the British High Commission in Kuala Lumpur, who tell me they are now dealing with the Malaysian authorities with a view to getting a more fitting memorial erected on the site.

~ * ~

Sources

a) Bibliography

The British in Malaya 1880-1941, by J.G. Butcher
British Rule in Malaya, by Robert Heussler
British Malaya: a Biographical Compendium, by Robert Heussler
Tales of the South China Seas, by Charles Allen
Out in the Midday Sun, by Margaret Shennan
20th Century Impressions of British Malaya, edited by A Wright & HA Cartwright.
Administering the Empire 1801 - 1968, by Mandy Barton
On Crown Service, by Anthony Kirk-Greene
An Eastern Cadet's Anecdotage, by Andrew Gilmour
Records of the British in Malaya and Singapore, by Alex Glendenning (article)
Sickness and the State (Malaya) by Leonore Manderson
Ah King & The Casuarina Tree - short story collections by W Somerset Maugham
Edwardian England, by Evangeline Holland
The Edwardians and Beyond, by Kate Juffs
The Gate Hangs High, by Mildred Coldwell
Pennine Valley, edited by Bernard Jennings (contributors included Leslie Goldthorp)
Marriage Law for Genealogists, by Rebecca Probert
The Genealogist's Internet by Peter Christian
Wills and Probate Records by Karen Glannum and Nigel Taylor

b) Websites

Numerous genealogy websites, especially: Ancestry *and* Find My
    Past
Numerous history sites, including: Join me in the 1900s.org.uk *and*
    Calderdale Companion
Malayan Newspaper Archives
British Newspaper Archives
Wikipedia
Met Office archives
www.timeanddate.com
Google maps
Malaysia Traveller
Lost Railways West Yorkshire.co.uk
Mike's Railway History/Malaya
www.britishtelephones.com
Fashion-Era.com
www.babycenter.com/names in Malaysia *and* baby development
various medical websites and some pregnancy and childbirth sites

Acknowledgements

Jonathan Moffat, Malayan Volunteers Group
David May, The War Graves Photographic Project
Beaulieu Motor Museum
Bordon Library Staff
Gordon Goldthorp
Keith Brignall